DEADLY CRIES

JENNA ST. JAMES

Deadly Cries

Jenna St. James

❧ 1 ❧

"It's freezing out here," Serena said before pulling her scarf up over her mouth and nose.

I scoffed. "That's because it's winter on Enchanted Island, dear cousin. And only three days until your wedding."

Tamara Gardener, Serena's best friend, laughed and looped her arm around Serena as we continued up the snowy sidewalk. "Not to worry. I'll keep your warm. That's probably one of my jobs as your maid-of-honor, right?"

Serena laughed. "Yes. Yes, it is."

"Speaking of warm," I said. "I love your new coat, Tamara."

Tamara lifted a gloved hand and touched the white fur around the hood of her black jacket. "Thank you, Shayla. I love it too. Betty's Boo-tique was having a massive winter sale last week. I went on the first day, which was a good thing. Betty told me she'd already sold over twenty of these coats. I even bought my mom one. I may have the same jacket as half the women on the island, but at least I'll be warm."

"What about me? What do I get to stay warm?" Needles whined from my shoulder. *"I'm so cold my wings can barely change colors! At this rate, I'll probably die of hypothermia."*

I rolled my eyes as Serena giggled.

"You're right," Serena said. "Needles can be a bit of a drama queen."

Huffing indignantly, Needles wrapped his wings around his body. *"I am not a drama queen. I am a two-hundred-year-old warrior. And sometimes this warrior gets cold!"*

"I still can't get over how some of you can hear Needles," Tamara said. "While a part of me is glad we left just minutes before the explosion, another part of me wishes I could hear Needles too."

Back in October, not only had my Bronco exploded, but it had exploded with Needles inside. He'd been badly wounded. One of the side effects of his injury had been the magical link that made it possible for my dad—Black Forest King—Zoie, and me to hear Needles, now made it possible for everyone else who was at the explosion to hear Needles…which drove my long-time boyfriend, Sheriff Alex Stone, absolutely crazy.

"If you didn't want to be out in this cold, Needles," I said, "you should have stayed back at the bakery with Mom, Mrs. Gardener, and Aunt Starla."

The three women had volunteered to keep the bakery open today while we did last-minute errands before the wedding. Normally, this was Serena's and Tamara's busiest time of the year, but with the wedding only days away, they'd cut back on their productivity. Most customers understood. After all, this was guaranteed to be the wedding of the year—or at least a tie for the wedding of the year.

The last wedding the islanders had attended was back in October after the Samhain festival when the eighty-year-old spinster twin witches, Opal and Pearl, had married the seventy-year-old bachelor twin witches, the Caraway boys.

"Is that Celeste's house across the street?" I pointed to the seafoam green cottage. "Fitting for a siren."

Serena giggled. "Wait until you meet her roommate. So *not* fitting for her."

While sirens were known for their musical abilities, not many of them made their living singing on the island. So when Serena heard Celeste Morningsong singing at the Earthly-Caraway wedding back in October, she knew she'd found her vocalist.

At first, Celeste had begged off, telling Serena she'd only performed at the wedding because the Earthly twins were customers at her yoga studio, Breathe Deeper, and Celeste was doing them a favor...but Serena was relentless. After weeks of pleading and plying Celeste with baked goods, Celeste said yes.

"I just want to check in and give her this gift," Serena said, shaking the box in her hand.

I laughed. "More baked goods? Pretty soon, the yoga teacher isn't going to be able to bend over and touch her toes."

Tamara giggled, and Serena sent me a mocking glare.

"Not baked goods, cousin," Serena said. "Just a thank-you gift. In case I don't get to see her before the ceremony. The yogis at Breathe Deeper aren't going to lose their leader."

We crossed the street and headed up the front walkway.

"Speaking of breathing deeper," I joked, "who's ready for the bachelorette party Friday night?"

Serena groaned. "It better not get out of control."

Tamara laughed and knocked on the door. "Is there any other way to be at a bachelorette party?"

"I'm ready for the bachelor party, if anyone cares," Needles said melodramatically.

The front door opened, and Celeste Morningsong smiled out at us.

"This is a nice surprise." She motioned us inside and pointed to the left, where the kitchen was located in the open-concept cottage. "I was getting ready to make something to drink. Just toss your coats over the couch."

We did as she directed, then crossed the room with her.

"I'm glad you caught me at home," Celeste said, snagging a couple cups from the cupboard. "Would you like coffee or hot tea?"

"Coffee," the three of us said simultaneously.

Celeste laughed. "How about Needles? Would he like something?"

"Hot buttered rum," Needles said. *"Heavy on the rum."*

Serena snorted, and I rolled my eyes.

"He's fine," I said, ignoring Needles' protests.

"I'm not due at the yoga studio until around ten," Celeste said. "That's when my first class is. Beginner yoga starts at eight." She shot us a grin. "Just a reminder."

"I wanted to drop off this gift in case things get too hectic at the wedding." Serena set the box down on the counter, which was littered with mail. "And I wanted to see how the songs were coming along?"

"That's so sweet of you," Celeste said. "Songs are memorized and ready to be sung."

Serena clapped her hands. "Yay. I'm so excited."

"I like your place," Tamara said as she accepted a mug from Celeste.

"Thanks. I've done most of the decorating. My roommate would live with bare walls and all black furniture if I let her." Celeste laughed, then staggered. Reaching out a hand to steady herself, she started to cough.

4

"You feeling okay?" I asked.

Celeste nodded. "Yes. Well, okay, not really. But not to worry, I'll be better before Saturday."

"What's wrong?" Serena asked. "Is it the flu or a cold?"

"Not sure. My energy level is low. I have some nausea, and I can't seem to stop sweating, even though it's near frigid in here."

A petite woman with black spiked hair and multiple ear piercings lumbered into the room. She had on black pajama bottoms and a t-shirt that read "Vampires Suck." She stopped, yawned loudly, then shuffled over to us.

"It's like the North Pole in here," the woman griped. "And wipe your mouth, Celeste. You're drooling."

Celeste gasped and swiped at her mouth. "Sorry. This is my roommate and best friend, Tabby Lefanger."

Tabby gave us a curt nod. "I'm telling you, Celeste, there's something wrong. More than just a cold or the flu."

"I'm about to have one of my vitamin boosters," Celeste said. "Would you like one?"

Tabby wrinkled her nose. "You know I hate that crap. The smell alone makes me want to hurl. I'll take my usual." She walked over to the coffee maker and poured a cup. "Hot coffee nice and black and dark." Took a sip of coffee and smiled. "Just like my soul." She glanced over at Celeste and scowled. "Sit down, Celeste. You look like you're about to keel over. You better get your butt in tonight, you hear?"

"Tabby works the night shift at the hospital," Celeste explained.

"Yes, please get better," Serena said. "Not just for my wedding, but because you really don't look well."

Celeste threw in a handful of chopped carrots, apples, and tomatoes into the blender, then added ice. Before securing the lid to the blender, she scooped out a large spoonful of green powder from a glass jar.

"What's that?" I asked.

"My own special blend." Celeste said. "I'm in the developing stages of marketing it. You can buy some at my studio. I have ground seaweed, dried and crushed kale, and a couple other secret ingredients in here." She added the powder and mixed the concoction in the blender before pouring it into a tall glass and gulping half of it down. "This should have me back on my feet in no time. I drink about three a day—morning, noon, and night."

"How're things with you and Brody?" Tamara asked. "Have you set a wedding date?"

"Oh, Shayla, listen to this," Serena said excitedly to me. "Celeste has had her own whirlwind romance. Just a few months ago, she met this guy, and he proposed like three weeks ago!"

Celeste set the glass down, her lower lip trembling. "Brody and I broke up last week."

"Oh, Celeste, I'm so sorry!" Tamara exclaimed.

"I'm sorry too," Serena added.

Celeste wiped away a tear. "It's okay." She frowned and took another drink of her health drink. "I should have known it wouldn't work out. Even though he was mostly a witch, he did have muse in him from his grandmother." She rolled her eyes, as though that should be explanation enough. "He just started being weird and pushy."

"Are you sure he isn't a gargoyle?" Needles demanded. *"Because I know for a fact that's how gargoyles behave."*

I narrowed my eyes at the mouthy porcupine resting on my shoulder.

"Why don't you open your present," Serena said. "That might make you smile."

6

Celeste finished the last of her drink, then set the glass on the counter. "Sounds good." She reached out to grab the box, but before she could touch it, her body started to shake and convulse. A few seconds later…she dropped to the ground.

🦋 2 🦋

"Celeste!" Tabby shouted, tossing her coffee mug into the sink, where it instantly shattered. "Someone call an ambulance!"

"I am," Serena said.

"Should a cold make her seize like that?" I asked.

"No," Tabby barked out, resting her head against Celeste's chest. "Her breathing is shallow. We need an ambulance now!"

I glanced over at the powder in the jar, then leaned down to sniff. I didn't smell anything off. It smelled like seaweed. Needles landed on the counter next to the jar and took a sniff for himself.

"Poison!"

"What?" Serena and I both shouted.

"Are you sure?" I demanded.

"I smell ground up water hemlock, Princess," Needles' wings were blue. *"Very deadly."*

I nodded. "Tabby, Needles says he can smell water hemlock."

Tabby's eyes went wide. "Water hemlock? That's lethal in

8

large amounts. Serena, tell the ambulance they need to have an IV ready to go. We suspect she's ingested water hemlock."

I pulled out my cell and called Alex.

"Hey," I said before he could talk, "I have a situation you might need to work if you're available."

"What's up?" he asked.

"I'm helping Serena and Tamara this morning with wedding things, and we went to Celeste Morningsong's house to go over wedding songs, and Celeste said she wasn't feeling well. Hadn't been feeling well for a few days now. She put a scoopful of this powder she makes herself in her veggie drink, and as soon as she finished drinking, she started seizing. Ambulance is on their way now. Needles smelled the jar, and he said there's water hemlock in the powder. Very poisonous."

"Grant and I are on our way. What's the address?"

I recited the address, then disconnected. Pacing back and forth, I thought about who might have done this to Celeste. My first suspect was the ex-boyfriend, Brody.

Since Celeste and Tabby lived in town, it didn't take but a couple minutes for the paramedics, Alex, and Grant to arrive.

"I filled Grant in on the way over," Alex said. "Anything more you've learned?"

I shook my head. "No. Celeste is still out, and Tabby won't leave her side."

"Let's take a look at this jar of poison," Alex said.

We headed over to where Needles was perched on the counter, next to the open jar.

"This jar is half-way gone," Needles said. *"She's ingested quite a bit of poison. Which makes sense when you think about her symptoms."*

"What symptoms?" Alex asked.

"Dizziness, nausea, lethargy, drooling, probably stomach

cramps," I said. "Depending on the dosage she was given will determine the severity of her symptoms. But we witnessed a few of them when we were talking with her."

Needles' wings turned blue. *"If she was drinking her health drinks three times a day and had a spoonful in each drink, I'd say she's ingested at least two days of the water hemlock. Maybe three."*

"So you think she was poisoned at the start of the week?" Alex mused.

"Makes sense," I said. "Celeste told us she has the drink three times a day. It would be an easy test for Finn to simulate and run to verify."

"Where is water hemlock found?" Grant asked.

"All over the island," I said. "But it's found primarily around rivers, ditches, and ponds."

"Any suspects?" Alex asked.

"I know she broke up with her fiancé last week," I said. "Other than that, I don't know of any."

"Why were you guys here again?" Alex mused.

I lifted the gift off the counter, and a piece of paper drifted to the floor. I set the gift down and bent to pick up the fallen note. "U no u want to sale." I flipped the note over, but there was no signature. I handed the note to Alex. "Here's something interesting."

"Not the best grammar," Alex mused. "But the intent is clear."

Using magic, I waved my hands and lifted the mail and other papers in the air so I could see them. "There are quite a few of these notes here."

"Bag them," Alex said. "We'll find out if Celeste or her roommate know who they're from, and then we'll have Finn run them for fingerprints, just in case."

Finn was the island's forensic scientist. She was so good at her job, supernatural laboratories all over the world wanted to recruit her. But she was perfectly happy on Enchanted Island.

I separated out all the notes and ended up bagging eight of them. The threats ranged from, "Sell now if you know what's good for you," to, "U better sell to me."

The ambulance had Celeste on the stretcher and was wheeling her out the door when Tabby turned to us.

"Can you please let her sister know what's happened?" she asked. "I want to ride to the hospital with Celeste, but her sister needs to know. She works at the yoga studio. She should already be there."

"I can do that," Alex said. "Just a quick question. Are these notes for Celeste? And do you know who sent them?"

Tabby rolled her eyes. "That lunkhead Garth Trollson leaves them on her windshield. He owns the gym next door to the yoga studio." She grabbed her jacket off the couch. "I need to go."

Without a backward glance, Tabby shoved her arms through the down jacket and slammed the door behind her…leaving Grant, Serena, Tamara, Alex, Needles, and me alone in the house.

"I know Tabby said to contact the sister," I said. "But do we know if Celeste has parents on the island?"

Serena shook her head. "The parents moved to the mainland to a fifty-and-over supernatural community about two years ago."

"We'll hold off calling them until we hear something more," Alex said. "Right now, I want to make sure we have all the threatening notes from this Garth Trollson."

"I'll check her bedroom," I said.

"We'll help," Serena added.

Serena, Tamara, and I headed toward the hallway. It didn't

take long to figure out which room was Celeste's. The first door I opened had burgundy walls, black curtains, and a black bedspread. There was a nightstand and lamp next to the bed, a couple candles, and a desk. Sparse and dark.

"Definitely doesn't scream Celeste," I said as I shut the door.

We hit the jackpot in the next room. The walls were a pale bluish-green, the bedspread a dark blue with coral pillows, and more girly knick-knacks than I'd ever seen in one place.

"I feel weird going through her drawers," Serena said.

"It's helping her," I said. "We want to find out who did this to her, and this is the best way."

"We're looking for notes?" Tamara asked.

I nodded. "But don't touch them." I handed them each an evidence bag. "If you find any, use your magic and levitate them into the bag."

Tamara took the closet, Serena the dresser, and I sat down on the bed and opened the nightstand. Dozens of folded papers caught my eye. Using magic, I levitated and read them.

"Whatcha find?" Tamara asked.

"Looks like love letters from her ex, Brody," I said.

"These look like they're from Brody as well," Serena said, levitating a couple notes in the air. "Only they aren't love letters. They range from anger to pleading. Basically, he was trying to get Celeste back."

"Let's bag these as well," I said. "You never know. They might come in handy to show intent or motive."

"I can't believe someone would purposely hurt Celeste," Serena said, "but I *really* hope it doesn't turn out to be the guy she almost married!"

I snapped pictures with my phone of the notes to keep as references, then gathered all the letters and headed back to the front room where Alex, Grant, and Needles sat talking.

"I was just telling Grant to take the rest of the day off," Alex said. "This was his last day anyway before the wedding, and he needs to be with you right now, Serena."

"Are you sure, Alex?" Grant asked. "Won't you and Shayla need help?"

"What am I?" Needles whined. *"Chopped liver?"*

"We can handle it," I assured Grant. "You can take my place with wedding prep, if that's okay?"

Serena bit her lip. "We did have more items on our list of things to do today. We still need to go by The Spellmoore and make sure everything is ready there. Then, I wanted to stop by Forever Flowers and check on how the flowers are coming. After that, maybe we could go to the hospital and check on Celeste?"

"You three go on and do that," Alex said. "Shayla, Needles, and I will run these items to Finn and see what she can tell us, then we'll go by the yoga studio."

"I'll drop my car off at Mom's," Serena said to Grant. "Can you pick up Tamara and me there?"

Grant nodded at his fiancée. "I can. And I'll run those evidence bags by the station for you, Alex. One less thing you have to do."

"Thanks," Alex said.

"If you're at the hospital and Celeste wakes up," I said, "or if she wakes up and they call you…"

"We'll let you know," Serena promised.

After they left, Alex and I did one last sweep, then locked the door behind us. We were almost at Alex's Blazer when a boy no older than six ran over to us. He was dressed in a red snowsuit that matched the red curls on his head.

"Hey! I'm Tucker. Don't tell my mom I'm out here, okay? I threw up last night, so she made me stay home from school today. Can you believe it? The last day of the school year, which

13

means cookies and treats and movies, and I have to stay home! Whoa! Is that a flying porcupine? Cool. What's his name?"

I smiled at the ease with which the boy fluttered from one subject to another. "He *is* a flying porcupine, and his name is Needles."

Needles shot up from my shoulder, did a twirl and bow, his wings throwing off myriad colors. The boy giggled and clapped.

"You better go on back inside," I said. "You don't want to get worse with the holiday around the corner."

Tucker shrugged. "I won't. I never get sick. I only threw up because of all the chocolate and soda floating around in my tummy. I went to visit Gammy last night, and she gave me lots of it as a secret."

Alex chuckled. "Sounds like a good Gammy."

The boy smiled, showing us his missing front tooth. "The best." He glanced over at the house. "Is Miss Celeste and Miss Tabby okay?"

"Do you know them?" I asked.

"Of course I do! Sometimes, I come over and play with them. Miss Celeste teaches me these funny poses to do with my legs and hands, and Miss Tabby likes to play tag. She can run really, really, *really* fast. Sometimes, I can't even catch her!" He shrugged, his thin shoulders jerking quickly. "But she's a vampire, so I guess that's normal. I'm a woodland fairy. I can't run as fast as Miss Tabby. Can Needles fly really fast?"

"He can," I said.

"Tucker," Alex said, "can you remember back to Monday? Just a couple days ago?"

Tucker scoffed. "Of course! I'm not a baby." He closed his eyes and scrunched his nose for a few seconds, then opened his eyes wide. "On Monday, I was at school until three. Came home, ate two cookies, went to the bathroom, played on my iPad, ate dinner, then Mom said I had to take a bath." Tucker rolled his eyes. "I just took one Saturday!"

Alex chuckled. "Did you notice anyone besides Miss Celeste and Miss Tabby hanging around the house on Monday or Tuesday?"

Tucker shook his head. "Not on Monday or Tuesday."

"Okay." Alex ruffled the boy's hair. "Thanks for helping out."

"But I did on Sunday," Tucker said.

My eyes met Alex's.

"You saw someone sneaking around Miss Celeste's house on Sunday?" I asked.

The boy nodded. "Yep. Some silly *girl*."

"How do you know it was a girl?" I asked.

"Because she had on a black coat, and it had this funny white stuff around the head part." He kicked at a patch of snow. "No boy would wear something like that."

Alex smiled. "Do you know who she was?"

"Nope. Never saw her before. She looked in the front window, then she went around back. I don't know what happened to her after that. I couldn't see her anymore."

"You've been a big help," Alex said. "Thanks for talking with us. You better go on back inside before your mom catches you out here."

"Okay." He gave us a wave. "See ya guys later. Bye Needles!"

"So now we have a mystery woman in a black coat to add to the list of suspects," I said as I climbed inside the vehicle. "That shouldn't be hard to find."

3

Breathe Deeper was located on Kraken Drive, just three blocks from the bakery. The parking lot was shared with the building next door, Trollson's Gym.

I stepped up onto the wooden front porch and opened the door to the studio. As I took a deep breath, myriad scents washed over me—lavender, sandalwood, patchouli, peppermint, cedarwood, and countless others.

"I love this smell," I whispered.

"Makes me sneeze," Needles griped from my shoulder.

The cute, dark-haired girl behind the counter quickly dropped the book she was reading onto her lap. "Hello. I'm LeeAnn Elmswood. Welcome to Breathe Deeper." She stood, shoved the book under a magazine on the counter, and smoothed back her hair. "How can I help you?"

"I'm Sheriff Stone, and this is Agent Loci. We'd like to speak to Celeste Morningsong's sister, please."

"Uh, okay. Her next appointment isn't for another hour, so I think she's available. I'll go check."

"Actually," Alex said, "if you'd just point us to where she is, that will be fine."

"Uh, okay." LeeAnn pointed to a door across the other side of the room. "Back there is where she does the massages. She should be in one of the rooms, cleaning."

I smiled and nodded to the girl. "Elmswood? Is your grandmother Willamina?"

"Yes."

"She's a member of my coven," I said. "Wonderful lady. I don't believe I've seen you, though. Do you practice at another coven?"

LeeAnn's cheeks turned pink. "I attend the singles coven." She rolled her eyes. "Much to my grandmother's displeasure."

I laughed and followed Alex into the back room.

"Hello?" he called out.

A woman who bore a striking resemblance to Celeste poked her head out of a room and frowned. "Hello. Sheriff? Is there something wrong?"

"We are here about Celeste," I said. "You're her sister, correct?"

The woman stepped out into the narrow hallway, her face suddenly tense. "Yes, I'm Chloe. Why? Is something wrong?"

"I'm afraid so," I said. "While visiting with your sister this morning, she suffered a seizure and was rushed to the hospital. Her roommate, Tabby, went with her."

Chloe clutched the doorframe, her face now deathly white. "Is she okay? What happened? Do you know anything?" She pushed herself upright. "I need to get to the hospital. My sister will need me."

"We haven't been given an update," Alex said. "We believe we know the cause of her seizure, but we need our forensic scientist to give us a definite answer."

"I need to go to her," Chloe whispered, wiping tears from her eyes.

"And we'll get you there as quickly as we can," Alex said. "But I really need to ask you a few questions. It's important we understand what happened to your sister."

Chloe nodded. "Right. Okay. But please hurry. Did she fall and hit her head? Why would she have a seizure?"

"Again, we are waiting on the tox reports to come back," Alex said, "but we believe we know enough to say it wasn't an accident. So we need to ask you some important questions."

"Not an accident?" Chloe shook her head. "I just don't understand."

"I was at Celeste's house when this happened," I said. "She is singing at my cousin's wedding this weekend. We'd stopped by to give her a gift and to see how the songs were coming along. While we were there, she whipped up a health drink and included a scoop of her vitamin booster."

Chloe gasped. "Her powder made her sick? How? She's been drinking it for almost six months now. She *swears* by it."

I glanced at Alex...who nodded at me. He was giving me the go-ahead to tell her what I knew. "We think maybe someone added something to her powder."

"What? I don't—I mean, I can't..."

Needles flew from my shoulder and hovered between Alex and me. "Needles is a gift from my father, Black Forest King. He has amazing talents, and one of them is identifying plants. He took a sniff of the powder, and immediately identified water hemlock."

Chloe gasped. "What? That's impossible. Poisonous plants? No way would Celeste put that in her drink. She's way too smart for that. Not even by accident! She knows her plants and herbs."

I nodded. "That's why we need to know if anyone had a

problem with Celeste. Has anyone been threatening her lately? Celeste told us she recently broke off her engagement with a man named Brody."

Chloe blinked, as though trying to focus on what I was saying. "Yes, that's true. I don't know exactly what happened because Celeste was very tightlipped about it. I *do* know he was angry when Celeste refused to put him in her will. Celeste owns this yoga studio, and I work here, but it's her business. Celeste's will states if she dies, then the yoga studio goes to me. Because they were going to get married, I guess Brody thought he deserved to be put in the will. I didn't think that was something to call off the wedding for, but every time I pressed for answers, Celeste closed up."

"While at Celeste's house," I said, "I found a piece of paper. It looked like a threatening note. It basically said she better sell the studio. Any idea who that was from?"

"Is Garth still sending her letters?" Chloe scowled. "That would be the guy next door. He owns the gym. He's been after Celeste to sell this place to him so he can knock down the wall and extend his gym. But that's not going to happen. I thought those notes had stopped. At least, that's what Celeste told me." She sighed. "I guess she didn't want me to worry."

"We'll be sure to speak to Garth next," Alex said.

Chloe nodded, then furrowed her brows. "Celeste said something odd to me the other night when we were drinking away her sorrows. She said Brody had money on her. I'm not sure what she meant because when I pressed, she said she didn't want to talk about it anymore. I don't know if it means something to you, but I just thought you should know."

"What's Brody's last name?" I asked.

"Lightweig."

"The guy who manages the taco place in town?" I mused.

"That's him."

Alex motioned to the three other doors. "Are all these massage rooms?"

Chloe shook her head. "The one at the end is where Celeste makes her soaps, body scrubs, essential oils, and the vitamin booster powder she puts in her drinks."

"Who all has a key to that room?" I asked. "I'm assuming it's locked?"

"Oh, yes," Chloe said. "It's always locked. I have a key, LeeAnn has a key, and Celeste has a key. That's it. Just the three of us."

"I hate to do this to you right now," Alex said, "but Shayla and I need to bag whatever jars are back there and take them to the lab. We need to make sure there's no poison in them like there may have been at her house."

Chloe's hands flew to her mouth. "You think someone poisoned her here? How?" She held up a hand. "No. Forget I asked. You just do what you need to do to find out who hurt my sister." She withdrew a key from her pocket and unlocked the door. Pushing it wide, she motioned us inside. "I just ask you please hurry. I really want to get to the hospital to see my sister. I need to shut down the diffusers in the other room, but I'll be right back to walk you out."

Using my magic, I threw up a light orb to illuminate the room. After a few seconds of casing where everything was, Alex and I found the area dedicated to Celeste's vitamin booster. Walking past the scrubs and soaps, we stopped at the bench filled with at least fifteen jars of the powder.

Alex flashed me a grin. "You're the witch. What do we do now?"

I grinned back at him. "Watch and be impressed."

Closing my eyes, I quickly conjured up evidence bags and two large baskets.

"Why the baskets?" Alex asked.

"Amateur question," Needles said, shaking his head.

I chuckled. "I'm not carrying all those evidence bags filled with glass jars out in my arms. I'd probably drop one. Shove them in a basket, and we're good to go."

Alex nodded. "Nice thinking."

It didn't take us long to collect the jars. We met up with Chloe in the hallway, and if she thought it odd we were carrying baskets, she kept it to herself. She simply locked the door and herded us back into the front of the studio, where LeeAnn sat reading her book.

"What's wrong, Chloe?" LeeAnn asked, setting her book down again. "Have you been crying?"

"It's Celeste," Chloe said. "She's at the hospital. I need to go to her."

"What?" LeeAnn jumped up from her stool. "The hospital? Is she okay? Was she in an accident on the way to work?"

Chloe shook her head and grabbed her purse behind the counter and gave LeeAnn a hug. "I'm headed to the hospital. Can you call my appointments and reschedule, then put on the supernatural website that classes for today will be cancelled?"

"Of course," LeeAnn said.

"Go ahead and shut down the studio after the current class is over and go on home."

LeeAnn nodded. "If you need me for anything, just call. Give my love to Celeste."

Chloe nodded and hurried out the door.

"I don't understand what just happened," LeeAnn said as she sat back down on her stool behind the counter.

"I'd like to ask you a couple questions," Alex said. "Do you know of anyone who would want to hurt Celeste?"

LeeAnn gasped. "Hurt her? Like she's…hurt?"

Alex nodded. "That's why she's at the hospital. Do you know of anyone who has been threatening Celeste lately?"

She shook her head. "Not really. I mean, I know she broke up with her fiancé, but Celeste was pretty quiet about why."

I frowned. "Anyone else? Anyone send her threatening notes or maybe harassing her?"

LeeAnn shrugged and glanced down at the floor. "Not that I can think of. I mean, sometimes she and Laurel Muser will get into spats." She held up the book she was reading when we first came into the studio. "That's why I have to hide this. I'm not supposed to read Laurel's stuff while I'm at work." LeeAnn's eyes went wide. "But I don't think Laurel would try to kill Celeste over it."

"Who is Laurel Muser?" Alex asked.

I snorted. "Only one of *the* most famous supernatural writers."

LeeAnn nodded. "And it's no secret that Laurel and Celeste do *not* get along."

❧ 4 ❧

"**T**otally different smell than the one next door," I muttered as Alex and I walked into Trollson's Gym.

"Smells like warriors train here," Needles said as he hovered near my face, pretending to fence with an imaginary opponent.

"You're both right," Alex said as he walked up to the counter where a perky blonde sat.

"Hello! My name's Amber. Welcome to Trollson's Gym. Oh! Sheriff Stone! And Shayla Loci! I recognize you from your uniforms and the gossip around town. Are you two looking to join?" She clasped her hands in glee. "This is wonderful! We have a free one-day trial upon signup."

Alex gave her a tight smile. "No, thanks. I'd like to speak to Garth Trollson, please."

Amber's smile slipped, but she didn't give up. "If you have questions about the membership, I'm sure I can answer them all. We have a family discount if—"

"Garth Trollson," Alex interrupted with just enough force to cause her smile to totally disappear.

"I'm afraid Mr. Trollson is busy," Amber said. "He's in the middle of his morning workout. He is to never be disturbed during this time."

Alex tapped the badge on his uniform. "Perhaps you don't understand what this means?"

Amber bit her lip, and she looked like she wanted to cry. "I know what it means! I just don't want to get in trouble for interrupting him. He's scary when he yells."

"How about I tell him Agent Loci and I pushed our way inside?" Alex said.

Amber nodded. "Okay. He's lifting in the weight room." She pointed through an open archway to the right. "Just go through there."

Three customers were running on treadmills, two more were on elliptical machines, and another six people were lifting weights on various equipment. It didn't take long to spot Garth Trollson—about six foot three, two hundred eighty pounds of pure muscle, short sandy hair, and a square, chiseled face. The fact he was sporting a Trollson's Gym t-shirt with the word "owner" on it didn't hurt with the identification, either.

"Mr. Trollson?" Alex mused as we stopped next to some kind of leg machine with tons of weights attached.

Trollson's eyes flickered over us, but he continued his leg lifts and ignored us.

"Mr. Trollson, I'm Sheriff Stone, and this is Agent Loci. We need to speak with you."

Trollson popped out an earbud. "Later. I'm lifting."

I raised my foot and pushed it against the weight he was lifting.

"Hey! What gives?" Trollson snapped. "I said later!"

I narrowed my eyes at him. "And I believe my partner said we needed to speak to you now."

Trollson snorted. "You think a little thing like you can keep a troll like me from lifting this weight? Move it, sister, before I fling you across this room."

Needles flew from my shoulder, his wings glowing bright red. I knew that look. But before I could say anything, Needles yanked two quills from his back and sliced up Garth Trollson's legs. Within seconds, blood appeared on the troll's shins and calves—the exact same color as Needles' wings. It took a moment for Trollson to react, but when he did, I was pretty sure his screams could be heard all the way across the island.

"Next time, I'll cut out your tongue, you insolent troll!"

I chuckled. "Needles says your tongue is next."

Glancing around, I could see we'd drawn the interest of the other weight lifters.

Alex sighed and crossed his arms over his chest. "Maybe we *shouldn't* let the porcupine cut up our suspect, Shayla?"

I shrugged. "You know Needles when I'm being threatened."

"This is police brutality!" Trollson cried, not caring that he was making a spectacle of himself in the middle of the gym.

"Technically," I said, "since I'm the game warden, it would be game warden brutality. And I guess Needles would fall under that umbrella as well." I shrugged. "Our duties are a little ambiguous."

Alex grinned, but he didn't tell me to back off.

I released my foot off the weight. "Now, Mr. Trollson, I believe my partner said we needed to speak to you."

Sighing, Trollson snatched his towel off the floor, wiped his face, then his legs, and motioned for us to follow him. I tried not to stare at his cut up tree-trunk legs flexing under his shorty-shorts as he walked, but I couldn't help it.

"I don't believe he has on undergarments," Needles hissed. *"This is highly inappropriate."*

I bit my lip to keep from laughing, but Alex nodded. "I agree with the porcupine."

"You agree with what?" Trollson demanded as he opened his office door and motioned us inside.

"Nothing," Alex said. "Mr. Trollson, we are here to ask you a few questions about Celeste Morningsong. You are aware of who she is?"

Garth Trollson rolled his eyes and lowered himself onto his leather chair. There wasn't a place for us to sit, so we stood in front of his desk. "Yeah, I know her. She's the siren who owns the little stretching place next door."

"It's a yoga studio," I said.

"Whatever. It's a waste of space, if you ask me."

"And that's why you want to buy it?" Alex asked. "So you can extend your gym?"

"Yeah. Why? What's going on? Did she complain about me to the police?"

"Do you recognize these notes?" I crossed behind his desk, got out my phone, and flipped through all of the notes. "Do you recognize those notes and those words?"

Trollson frowned, and then shrugged. "I guess. I mean, I guess I recognize some of them."

"We found these notes at Celeste's house this morning," I said.

"Yeah? And so what? She knows I'm leaving them for her."

"A person might see these as threats," I said.

"They ain't threats," Trollson insisted.

"Really?" I said. "Let me read these to you. 'Sell now if you know what's good for you,' and 'U better sell to me.' Those don't sound like threats?"

"I've offered the siren market value for that building. I don't understand why she doesn't sell to me. She can move her stretching class somewhere else."

I narrowed my eyes. "It's a yoga studio."

"Whatever. Is that what this is about? She called you guys because I've left a couple notes on her windshield, reminding her she can sell to me?"

"A couple?" I said. "Try over ten."

Trollson frowned. "Oh, okay. I didn't realize it was that many, but so what? There ain't no law saying I can't offer to buy her place from her every day if I want."

"It's your word choice," I snapped. "It's borderline harassing and threatening. And we *can* arrest you for that."

Trollson crossed his arms over his massive chest, and for a second, I thought the t-shirt might rip from his biceps. "Am I under arrest?"

"No," Alex said. "We just wanted to establish you are the person who sent Celeste Morningsong these notes."

"Okay. And why?"

"Early this morning, Ms. Morningsong was rushed to the hospital. Early signs point to poisoning."

"What?" Trollson leaped from his chair. "I didn't poison no one! I mean, I might have sent a couple notes, but I didn't hurt the girl. It's not in my nature."

I snorted. "Less than a minute ago, you threatened to toss me across the gym."

"Just words! I didn't really mean it. And, like I told you guys, my notes, they ain't threats! Look, I'm sorry to hear someone tried to kill her, but it wasn't me." He lowered himself back into his chair. "Although, now might be the perfect time to call the sister and see if Celeste might want to sell."

"I wouldn't advise it," Alex said.

There was just enough coldness in Alex's words, that the troll actually paused.

"I was just thinking aloud, man," Garth Trollson said, a fake smile plastering his face. "Didn't say I was actually going to do it."

Alex nodded. "Right."

"Look, you're wasting your time with me. You should question her boyfriend—or ex-boyfriend if the rumors are true. I saw them fighting out front last week when I was coming to work."

"Did you overhear anything?" Alex asked.

"I heard the guy begging her to change her mind. I also heard the words 'you die' when I walked by. Now, if that doesn't sound suspicious, I don't know what does."

"He has a point," Needles said.

"One last question," Alex said. "Are you aware Celeste has a vitamin booster she puts in her drinks?"

Troll grunted. "Oh, yeah. She tried to get me to sell that junk in my gym. I told her absolutely not. My clients don't go in for frou-frou. They want *real* protein drinks."

❦ 5 ❦

I clicked my seatbelt and turned to Alex. "He admitted to putting the notes on Celeste's car, *and* he has motive to want her dead."

"The big question is, how did Trollson get the water hemlock into the jar Celeste was using at her house?"

Needles piped up from the backseat. *"He gave it to one of his arm muscles, and they just flexed it in."*

Alex laughed as I turned around and tossed Needles a large pretzel stick.

"Once Finn can give us the approximate time the poison was added," Alex said, "we should be able to narrow our questions better."

I glanced at the dashboard clock. "Hopefully, we'll hear from Finn within the next couple hours."

Howling Good Tacos & Nachos was packed with holiday shoppers stopping to fuel up before heading to the next store. We stood in line for twenty minutes before finally giving the guy behind the counter our order.

"It will be about ten minutes," he said, handing us a number and our empty cups. "We'll call your number when it's ready."

"Thank you," Alex said. "We also need to speak to Brody Lightweig, please."

"Uh, sure, Sheriff." The young man pushed a button under the counter. "He should be here shortly."

We moved down to the far end of the counter, where two other customers waited for their food.

"You know, Princess," Needles said as he landed on my shoulder. *"I did just have to defend your honor. I should be rewarded with a nice salty margarita."*

"Dream on," I muttered.

When Brody Lightweig stormed out from the back kitchen, Alex raised his hand to get Brody's attention. Shock and something else passed over Brody's face before he schooled his features and walked over to us.

Running his hands through his brown hair, he gave us a winning smile. He was boyishly handsome with soft features. I put him in his early thirties.

"May I help you? Was there a problem with your order, Sheriff?"

Alex shook his head. "Brody Lightweig?"

"Yes."

"I'm Sheriff Stone, and this is Agent Loci. Is there a place we can go for more privacy?"

I surreptitiously glanced at a young girl who had been wiping down the same spot on the counter for about two minutes now. She wasn't doing a very good job at pretending to be uninterested.

"I'm busy, Sheriff," Brody said. "This is about as private as we're going to get."

"You know Celeste Morningsong?" Alex asked.

"I do."

"When was the last time you saw or spoke to Celeste?" Alex asked.

Brody scowled. "I dunno. Maybe a week ago when she suddenly broke it off with me. Why?"

"You haven't tried calling her?" I probed when I saw the girl's head jerk up at Brody's answer. "Haven't gone by her place? No contact whatsoever?"

Brody shrugged. "That's what I said. Why? Is she saying I did something?"

I glanced over at the girl, but she quickly averted her eyes and continued to wipe the counter.

"Earlier this morning," Alex said, "Celeste may have ingested what we believe to be poison. She's at the hospital right now."

No surprise or shock or emotion of any kind showed on Brody's face. "She's alive?"

"Yes," I said. "You don't seem surprised."

Brody shrugged. "She's not my fiancée anymore. Why should I care?"

I narrowed my eyes. "Do you know of anyone who would want to hurt Celeste?"

Brody snorted. "That Neanderthal who owns the gym next door was always giving her grief. You should try talking to him."

"We did," Alex said. "I assume you know about the vitamin booster Celeste makes?"

Brody frowned. "You mean that seaweed junk? Yeah, I've seen it. She drinks like three glasses of that gross stuff every day."

"She makes it herself, right?" I asked.

"Yeah."

I nodded. "Do you know where she makes it?"

Brody shrugged. "I think she makes it at her yoga studio. She also sells it there, and then she takes home jars for herself." He glanced at his watch. "If that's all the questions you have, I need to get back to work."

"Not quite," Alex said. "We know one of the issues you had with Celeste was that she wouldn't put you in her will for inheritance of the yoga studio upon her death. We also heard from a witness that you 'had some money on her.' What does that mean?"

"I have no idea," Brody snapped.

Alex smiled. "No problem. I'm sure Celeste can clarify what that means when I see her at the hospital later today."

Brody's nostrils flared. "Can I go?"

"Of course," Alex said. "Thank you for your time."

Brody whirled around and stalked back into the kitchen. The eavesdropping girl looked at me, then quickly averted her gaze again.

"You see her, right?" I whispered.

"Yeah," Alex said. "But I don't think she'll talk right now. Let's eat here and see what happens."

Needles laughed. *What happens is we'll get nice and full.*

A few minutes later, our order number was called.

"We've decided to eat here," Alex told the eavesdropping girl. "That's okay, right?"

The girl nodded. "Yes, sir." She cleared her throat. "I can fill your drinks for you and bring them over."

I handed her our empty cups and smiled. "That would be great. Thank you."

We sat down at the table farthest from the counter and next to a window. It wasn't long before the girl approached our table, carrying our drinks. With her back to the counter, she slowly placed our drinks in front of us.

"I know you want to tell us something," I whispered. "Anything you say is confidential."

The young girl bit her lip. "I don't want to get in trouble and get fired, but I think you should know something." She glanced quickly behind her. "What Brody told you wasn't true. About seeing his ex. My grandfather, Max Longwolf, is a mail carrier for the island. He knows Brody is my boss, so he told me this story, thinking it was kind of funny. He had no idea that Celeste and Brody had broken up."

"What did he tell you?" I asked.

"He said he saw Brody looking in Celeste's front window on Monday. Grandpa thought maybe he'd lost his key and was locked out of the house. He was going to roll down his window and give Brody a hard time, but then he said he saw Tabby driving up the road. He figured she would let him in, so he just drove away." She cleared her throat. "So when Brody said he hadn't been to Celeste's house in over a week, that wasn't true."

6

"I'm so full," Needles bellyached as he plopped down in the backseat. *"I need a nap. Try not to talk too loud."*

"We'll try," I said dryly before turning my attention back to Alex, who was pulling out onto the street. "We know Brody lied to us about the last time he had an interaction with Celeste. We also know one of the things he fought with Celeste about was not being included in her will. So he has motive and opportunity."

My cell phone dinged, and I read the incoming text.

"It's from Grant. He says Celeste is awake but still in and out of consciousness. Might be a good time to talk with her. She's on the third floor."

Alex made a U-turn and headed toward Wand Avenue, where the hospital was located. Since Needles was fast asleep in the back, we left him inside the Blazer.

We got off the elevator on the third floor and headed toward the room number Grant had given me. Before we could reach the room, Tabby called my name from the nurses station.

"I'm not sure if she's awake," Tabby said. "I just checked on her, and she was sleeping. Grant, Serena, and Tamara are in the waiting lounge."

"I have a quick question to ask," Alex said. "Did you work Monday?"

"You mean this past Monday? A couple days ago? No."

"I have a witness who states they saw someone peering into your windows on Monday," Alex said. "When this individual went to confront the person who was peeping inside, he saw your car coming down the street. He figured you could handle it."

It wasn't the entire truth, but enough of the story Tabby should be able to respond.

"I *did* go out around one. I needed to run to The Craft & Candle to pick up some items. When I got halfway there, I realized I forgot my wallet. So I turned back around, went home and got my wallet, then returned to the store."

"So you never saw anyone near your house?" Alex asked.

"No, but I wasn't really looking for anyone, either. I was focused on getting my wallet." She bit her lip. "Are you thinking someone broke in and that's when they dumped the poison into Celeste's jar?"

"It's a theory," Alex said.

"I'm so mad at myself!" Tabby hissed. "I should have paid more attention. It was that creep, Brody, wasn't it?" She scowled at the wall. "When I get my hands on him!"

"We aren't at liberty to say who it was," I said. "So don't jump to conclusions."

Even though she was completely right.

Tabby sighed. "I'm sorry. I'm just upset. Just so you know, Dr. Witcher and Dr. Cauldron have both been treating Celeste. Magic-infused herbs and IVs are attacking the poison. They believe she'll make a full recovery, but she'll be asleep for the next twelve hours or so."

"That's wonderful," I said. "We won't stay long. Just long enough to check on her."

Tabby nodded and squeezed my arm. "Thank you. I'm so grateful Needles was with you this morning. By the time Celeste fell to the floor, my mind was focused on four possible reasons for her seizure, and none of them included poison. Needles helped save her life."

"I'll let him know," I said.

Alex and I continued down the hallway until we reached Celeste's room. Pushing open the door, I smiled at Chloe sitting in a chair next to the bed.

"She just fell back asleep," Chloe whispered.

There were myriad clean-air plants of various sizes sitting on shelves and on the floor, large windows letting in natural light, and soft spa music pumping through a speaker high on the wall.

"This is lovely," I said. "I haven't really been inside the hospital much."

"Me, neither," Chloe said. "It's amazing the way they intermingle a little supernatural with medicine."

"Thank you," Celeste whispered.

We all glanced down at the pale woman in the bed.

"You awake, little sister?" Chloe asked.

"Hhmmm," Celeste replied.

"Celeste," I said, "can I ask you a quick question? We know Brody was upset because he wasn't being written into your will, but is that the only reason why you broke up?"

Celeste forced her eyes open, shaking her head.

"Okay," I said. "What did you mean when you told your sister Brody had money on you?"

Celeste's eyelashes fluttered closed, and for a second, I thought she wouldn't answer.

"Leo. Highwolf. Policy."

I glanced over at Chloe, but she just shrugged.

"Are you saying..." My voice trailed off when I realized Celeste had fallen back asleep.

"Do you have any idea what she's talking about?" I asked.

Chloe shook her head. "No. She never told me specifics."

"Leo Highwolf?" Alex mused. "Isn't he the insurance guy over on Mystic Drive?"

"Yep," I said. "And we might want to go talk to him before he closes his business for the holidays."

"Thank you," Chloe whispered. "The doctors have said they've treated the poison and she should make a full recovery. But I also want to say thank you for trying to find out who hurt Celeste."

I gave Chloe a hug, and Alex and I walked over to the visitor's lounge. Grant, Serena, and Tamara were sitting in the chairs.

"We just came from seeing Celeste," I said. "She looks good. I heard she's going to make a full recovery."

"Thank the goddess," Serena said.

"Do you need any help with the investigation?" Grant asked.

"Nope," Alex said. "Shayla and I have this under control. You guys focus on what still needs to be done before the wedding."

Serena bit her lip. "Well, I do need to run out to The Spellmoore and speak to Melody still."

Grant nodded. "Then Tamara and I will go with you."

"Not to worry," Alex said, "Shayla and I will keep you guys apprised of what's going on. Right now, try to enjoy this time before your big day."

7

"**G**ood afternoon," a thirty-something woman with red hair and green eyes greeted Alex and me as we strolled through the front door of Highwolf Insurance. "How may I help you?"

"We need to speak to Mr. Highwolf," Alex said.

"Who may I tell him is calling?" she asked.

"Sheriff Stone and Agent Loci."

"Just one moment." The attractive woman spoke into her phone, then stood. "If you'll follow me."

With a toss of her hair, she sashayed down the hallway and knocked on the door.

"Come in," a deep voice called.

Leo Highwolf was six feet tall, muscular, and had wide shoulders and narrow hips. He looked more like a bodyguard than an insurance guy.

"What's with all the Herculean men?" Needles asked as he hovered above my shoulder. *"You feeling intimidated, Gargoyle?"*

Alex gave Needles an icy stare, but he didn't rise to Needles' bait.

"Afternoon, Sheriff. Agent Loci. And this must be Needles. He's the talk of the island." Leo clapped his hands together. "What can I do for you today?"

Highwolf's secretary shut the door behind us as Highwolf motioned for us to sit down across from him.

"My partner and I have a few questions for you," Alex said. "Early this morning, Celeste Morningsong was poisoned. She's recovering at the hospital right now, but when I questioned her about insurance policies, she mentioned your name and Brody Lightweig's name."

"My goodness!" Highwolf exclaimed. "I'm sorry to hear this. I hope she's okay?"

"She should make a full recovery," Alex said. "But you understand my concern when she mentioned Brody's name and an insurance policy, correct?"

"If you are implying that Brody Lightweig poisoned Celeste for the life insurance money, I have a hard time believing that."

I crossed my arms over my chest. "Why is that?"

"Because they're engaged to be married," Highwolf said. "Or, at least they were a few weeks ago when he came in here to speak to me."

"And what did he speak to you about?" Alex asked.

Leo Highwolf frowned. "I don't know how comfortable I am telling you about my client's policy."

"I'll mention this again," Alex said. "Agent Loci and I are investigating what is looking more and more like an attempted murder. The victim mentioned you and an insurance policy with regard to her *ex*-fiancé. Notice the emphasis on 'ex' I just made?" Alex gave him a small smile. "Now do you feel comfortable telling us about the policy?"

Highwolf sighed. "Of course. I'm sorry. About two weeks ago, Brody came in to talk about taking out an insurance policy on his fiancée, Celeste. He said he was about to invest a heavy chunk of money into Celeste's studio and health drink, but he wanted to make sure if something ever happened to her that he would see his investment back. This is a standard practice in many businesses. Partners taking out insurance on the other partner."

"And how much was this policy for?" I asked.

"One hundred thousand dollars," Highwolf said.

Needles whistled. *"That would buy me a lot of pretzels."*

"Again, well within reason," Highwolf said quickly.

"And this is legal?" I asked. "Taking out an insurance policy on another person?"

Highwolf nodded. "Yes, ma'am. It's perfectly legal. Like I said, a lot of partners do it for business purposes."

Alex stood and held out his hand. "Thank you for your time, Mr. Highwolf. If we have any more questions, we'll be in touch."

"Of course. I hope Celeste makes a full and speedy recovery."

"One hundred thousand dollars is a huge motive to kill," Needles said as we exited Highwolf's office and headed to the main lobby.

"Enjoy the rest of your day," the secretary called as we walked outside.

"I think—"

I was interrupted by the text notification that sounded from Alex's phone.

"It's Finn," he said. "She has everything ready for us."

"Perfect," Needles said. *"I could use another nap."*

* * *

P earl Earthly-Caraway sat behind her desk, giggling into the phone. When she saw Alex and me, she whispered she needed to go and dropped the phone back onto the receiver.

"Good morning, Sheriff. Agent Loci. Isn't it a fine morning?" Pearl gushed.

This new Pearl was still hard for me to get used to. Ever since she'd gotten married, the octogenarian had been in one continuously good mood. A complete one-eighty from her normal dragon-like demeanor.

"It *is* a fine morning," I said. "How is Mr. Caraway doing?"

Pearl giggled, and I couldn't help the grin that spread over my face. "He's wonderful, dear. Especially now that Opal and I have perfected the Prolong Spell."

Alex's brows furrowed. "The Prolong Spell? What's that?" He turned to me. "Is it legal?"

I let out a bark of laughter. "I'll tell you later. Pearl, can we go see Finn?"

"Yes, yes." Pearl waved her hand in the air, then grabbed the phone. "I better check on my love."

"Never mind," Alex mumbled as we headed down the hallway. "I get what the Prolong Spell is now. I thought she was trying to prolong her husband's *life*, not his stamina."

I laughed. "It's the magical equivalent to the little-blue-pill humans have."

"I get it. No need to explain further." Alex knocked once on Finn's door to her laboratory, then pushed it open.

"Merry meet, crime solvers," Finn called out from behind her computer. "C'mon over, and I'll fill you in on what I've learned so far."

Alex and I crossed over to her cluttered workspace and leaned against her counter.

"I have confirmed the poison *is* water hemlock," Finn said, "and the jars taken from the yoga studio did *not* have poison inside them, just the one at Celeste's house."

"So it would reason," I said, "that the poison was added at her house, and not at the yoga studio."

Alex nodded. "I'd agree. If the would-be killer added it at the studio, anyone could have bought the vitamin booster since Celeste sells it there. The poisoner wanted to make sure only Celeste ingested the poison."

"I also did some experiments," Finn said. "Adding the same amount Celeste added three times a day, it looks like the poison was added to the jar either Sunday or Monday."

I glanced at Alex. "We know Brody was sniffing around Celeste's house on Monday."

"We do," he said. "Plus, we know an unidentified woman was seen at the house on Sunday. I'd like to know where the other suspects were on Sunday and Monday, now that we have a timeline."

"What about fingerprints?" I asked.

"Nope. Sorry. The culprit must have been wearing gloves."

"That's fine," Alex said. "Garth Trollson already admitted to writing the notes." Alex rapped his knuckles on the counter. "Thanks, Finn. You're the best."

She gave Alex a salute, and we exited the laboratory. Since Pearl was still giggling into the phone, I just lifted my hand and waved. She didn't even notice.

"Did you find out anything helpful?" Needles spread his wings wide—the equivalent of a stretch—as Alex and I hopped inside the Blazer.

"Sure did," I said. "We know the water hemlock was added to Celeste's jar at her house either on Sunday or Monday."

Needles smacked his lips together. *Isn't that nice? Now, I could use some salt. How about a pretzel, Princess?"*

I rummaged around in my bag and tossed him a large pretzel. He snatched it out of the air with his paw and went to town.

"Should we go see Brody and confront him?" I asked.

"No." Alex pulled out his cell phone. "I'm sending Deputy Sparks out to Trollson's Gym. I want him to get Garth's alibi for Sunday and Monday."

"So we're gonna let Brody stew a little? I like it."

Alex laughed and typed Laurel Muser's name into his new police-sync app the IT forensic scientist, Gordon Hoots, had developed for the sheriff's department. No longer did we have to rely on calling in to find out where people lived. Gordon had mapped out the entire island and had his equally talented code-writing nephew, Jordan Owlman, design an app.

Alex glanced at the address on the screen, then turned left onto the busy street. "Let's go see what Laurel Muser can tell us."

🌺 8 🌺

L aurel Muser lived five miles north of town on Ghostly Lane. According to GiGi, Laurel's two-story expansive stone home with two turrets was a recent build.

"I take it book sales are good," Alex murmured.

I laughed. "Laurel is a muse. They are known for their prowess in literature, arts, and sciences."

"So you know this woman?" Alex asked.

"Nope. Never had the pleasure of meeting her. She doesn't go out often, from what I've been told."

"Muses are not to be trifled with lightly, Princess," Needles said from my shoulder. *"Countless stories have been told throughout history of their cunningness."*

Alex knocked on the wooden door, then pressed the doorbell. A few seconds later, I heard the click-clack of high heels inside. A striking woman with icy-blonde hair cut in a bob just under her chin smiled out at us, giving me a glimpse of white teeth. Her plum-colored lipstick matched her plum pantsuit.

"May I help you?" She gave our uniforms the once over. "I take it you are not here for an autograph?"

"No, ma'am. I'm Sheriff Stone, and this is Agent Loci. We need to speak to you about Celeste Morningsong."

Laurel scoffed and rolled her blue eyes. "Now what? Did she call the police station on me? How absolutely juvenile."

I cocked an eyebrow. "Did she have a reason to call the sheriff's station on you?"

"You might as well come in and sit for a spell," Laurel said. "If we are going to discuss Chloe and Celeste Morningsong and their bias against me, then we might as well do it in comfort."

We followed her across the tiled foyer and through a massive arched doorway to the left. Floor-to-ceiling bookshelves lined all four walls, and I couldn't help but smile at the rolling wooden ladders assigned to each bookshelf. It was all very *Beauty and the Beast*.

"This is my writing room," Laurel said. "Go on. Have a look around."

My eyes were immediately drawn to the framed, life-size posters of Laurel's books recessed inside some of the shelves. I recognized the covers, even though I'd never read any of the books.

"As you can see, with nearly every book release, I've hit either the *ST* bestseller list or the *SUSA Today* bestseller list."

"Is that the same list you tell me I'm on sometimes when I piss you off, Princess?" Needles snickered.

Alex chuckled, then tried to cover it by coughing. "I apologize. I'm afraid I don't know what any of those lists are."

Laurel raised one perfectly groomed eyebrow. "Let me enlighten you, Sheriff. *ST* bestseller means *Supernatural Times* bestseller, and *SUSA Today* is *Supernatural USA Today* bestseller." She tossed her head, then somehow managed to look down her nose at Alex. "It is what every author strives for, I assure you."

While I couldn't care less one way or the other if she had some title or letters attached to her name, I guess some people might. I looked at Needles, hovering near a bookshelf, and I could tell by the way he closed his eyes and snored softly that he was equally unimpressed. I pursed my lips together to keep from smiling. The little rascal's wings wouldn't be moving if he were really asleep.

"That's all very nice and impressive," Alex said, "but I'm afraid we are not here to talk about your books, Ms. Muser. We need to discuss Celeste Morningsong."

Laurel waved her hand in the air, motioning for us to sit. Walking around her massive desk, she sat down in a red leather chair. Reaching out, she closed her laptop, and I couldn't help but wonder if she was working on another book.

"You may call me Laurel." She leaned back in her chair and shook her head. "Celeste Morningsong has been a thorn in my side ever since she opened that yoga studio—both she and her sister, really." She sighed. "As I'm sure you both are aware, muses and sirens do not get along. History proves our superiority." Her eyes flashed, and I could see temper rolling just under the surface. "I have tried on countless occasions to visit the yoga studio, but I never even get in the front door." Laurel gripped the sides of her chair so tightly, her knuckles were white. "Imagine barring *me* from a yoga studio?"

"I'm afraid you've lost me," Alex said. "I don't know of a feud between muses and sirens."

Even though I knew about the historical feud, I didn't say anything. I wanted to hear Laurel's take.

Laurel gasped. "What do they teach in supernatural schools nowadays? There are actually many stories regarding various supernaturals who have tried to challenge muses and each has lost." She leaned forward and rested her arms on her desk. "However, I will stick with the sirens. Many, many years ago, a group of sirens challenged the muses to a singing contest. Simply put, the sirens lost, and they've hated us ever since." She smiled. "Did you know there's even a marble sarcophagus at the Metropolitan Museum of Art in New York which depicts this challenge? The silly humans view it as myth, but I can assure you, it is fact."

"Guess we know why Laurel and Celeste don't get along," Needles said from my shoulder.

"Are you aware," Alex said, "that early this morning, Celeste Morningsong was poisoned with water hemlock and rushed to the hospital?"

Laurel's eyes widened. "I was not. Is she alive?"

"She's very much alive," I said.

"That's too bad," Laurel said. "I won't pretend to be sorry. It would be a lie, and I'm sure you are both superior at your jobs and would know immediately I was lying."

"Do you know where Celeste Morningsong lives?" Alex asked.

Laurel snorted. "It's not a big island, Sheriff. Of course I know where she lives. What I haven't told you is that I was trying to put aside these petty issues with Celeste and her sister. After all, Celeste was dating my second or third cousin." She flashed us a grin. "Did you know that? Brody is mostly a witch, but his great-great grandmother *was* a muse."

"We didn't know that," I said. "Thank you for telling us."

"That's why I thought this last time I tried to get a membership to the studio that Celeste would allow it." She shrugged. "But no. I was denied entrance."

I nodded. "I can see why you'd be upset. Do you know of

anyone who had an issue or problem with Celeste Morningsong?"

Laura let out a small bark of laughter. "You mean besides me? Well, I have heard that the owner of the gym next door has left her threatening notes. Or at least, that's the rumor Brody told me."

"Can you account for your whereabouts this past Sunday and Monday?" Alex asked.

"I'm on a deadline, Sheriff. That means I'm pretty much chained to my laptop. I was home both days…all day and all night."

"Can anyone vouch for you?" I asked.

Laurel shook her head. "I'm afraid not. Well, I did have contact with my editor a couple times by phone, but that was only a few minutes each time."

Alex stood, and I followed suit.

"Thank you for your time," I said. "If you can think of anything that might help us in our investigation, please don't hesitate to call the station. And if we have any more questions for you, we know where to find you."

"Just a moment." Laurel scribbled something down on a piece of paper, then handed it to me. "That's my lawyer's number. If you have any more questions, you can contact him. I was gracious enough to entertain you today, but I'm sure you understand when I say I'm done answering questions without him. I must protect my name and my brand."

9

"This is nice paper." I rubbed the paper with the attorney's name and number between my fingers, then folded it in half and stuck it in my wallet before clicking on my safety belt. "So for Laurel's motive, we have a life-long feud historians and artists both depict, and anger at Celeste for not letting her join her yoga studio. Plus, we know Laurel and Brody are distantly related. Are we going back to question Brody now?"

"Not yet. I want to do that tomorrow morning at his home. Throw him off his game. If we can get inside his house, we might see something of interest."

"This is Zoie's last day of school before the holiday break, right?"

Alex nodded. "It is."

"Is she going out tonight with Brick?"

Alex's daughter, Zoie, had been seeing boyfriend Brick for months now, and it seemed to be going well. But Brick was a senior and looking to the future, which I knew made Zoie nervous.

49

"Yes," Alex said, "they're going out. I guess the theater is playing some Italian movie called *The Legend of the Christmas Witch*. After grabbing a bite at the café, they're going to the show."

I gave him a slow smile. "How about you come out to my place for dinner? Zoie has loaded me down with some of her favorite foods. I can pull something out of the freezer, and then we can gorge on the rejects Serena sent me yesterday."

Alex laughed. "Rejects?"

"Desserts she's not serving for one reason or another at her wedding. A cookie might be darker than she liked, one of the cupcakes didn't frost perfectly, just silly things like that. I have more goodies than I know what to do with."

"Even I'm turning a little green at the thought of consuming more sugar," Needles grumbled. *"A porcupine needs more salt in his diet, not sugar."*

I turned and laughed at Needles' scrunched face and green wings.

"Sounds good to me," Alex said. "We can go over our completed list of suspects, motives, and alibis."

"My Bronco is in front of the bakery." I glanced at the clock on the dashboard. "It's four now. Why don't you come out around seven? I need to go home and visit Dad real quick."

* * *

I laced up my sneakers, zipped up my winter running jacket, and donned my hat and gloves. The temperature had dropped another ten degrees in the hour I'd been home. But the lasagna was in the oven, and I still wanted to see Dad... cold weather notwithstanding.

"A porcupine could freeze to death out here," Needles whined from inside the hood of my jacket.

"You could have stayed behind," I reminded him as I jogged down the path that would lead me to Black Forest.

Light snow flurries had started to fall about thirty minutes ago, and while the thickness of the trees helped to shield me for the most part, I was eager to get inside Black Forest and feel the warmth the magic would supply.

A half-mile later, I saw the swarm of fireflies headed my way... their lights illuminating the surrounding snow. It was breathtaking.

"We are excited about Serena's wedding!"

"Why didn't Alex Stone come with you?"

"Is it true GiGi is marrying Serena and Grant?"

"Will you bring us nectar for the Yule celebration?"

Needles popped out from my hood. *"Give the princess some room. She's had a hard day. Stop smothering her."*

I stopped in front of the large pine tree and waited patiently for him to lift his branch and let me pass.

"Princess," the old pine said, *"so lovely to see you. Please enter. Black Forest King is eagerly awaiting you."*

I ducked under the massive branch and entered Black Forest —the most magical place I'd ever been. And being an apprehension agent in the Paranormal Apprehension and Detention Agency meant I'd been to a lot of magical places. Nothing compared to the feeling inside Black Forest.

I stood and just let the peace and tranquility flood my body before taking off after Needles, who'd zipped on ahead of me once we were inside the forest. Like me, Needles always got an instant charge when we crossed the threshold.

It didn't take long before I saw my dad.

A Genius Loci...and the most magnificent tree I'd ever seen.

His tree roots were at least four feet tall and extended out of the ground about twenty feet from the base of the tree. His trunk was one hundred twenty feet around, and his branches—which averaged about thirty to forty feet—were strong and thick.

"Daughter of my Heart," Dad's voice rumbled inside my head. *"So lovely to see you tonight. I was worried the snow might keep you away."*

I jumped up onto his roots and ran down the length of him before stopping and giving his trunk a hug. "Hey, Dad." I plopped down at his base and leaned my back against him. "A little snow isn't going to keep me away. How are things in the forest?"

"Things are well. How about you? How are things on the island?"

"The island is good. Unfortunately, one of the citizens isn't. Serena, Tamara and I were visiting a siren who's supposed to sing at the wedding, and someone poisoned her with water hemlock! Luckily, Needles was there, and he identified the poison for us, so she received the help she needed. She's still in the hospital being treated by two witches, but they expect her to recover. So now Alex and I are trying to find out who did it and why."

"I am happy to hear she will be okay. And that Needles was of help to you."

Needles' gold and silver wings fluttered near my face. *"I'm always of help to the princess."*

I scoffed. "Always? Let's not get ridiculous."

Dad laughed. *"I am sure you are, old friend."*

Needles stuck his tongue out at me, then flew off into Dad's tree branches.

"Will things proceed with Serena's wedding?"

"Yeah. There are still a couple more days before the wedding, so hopefully Celeste will make a full recovery by then and be able to sing. Tomorrow is Yule and the winter solstice, so we decided to do the wedding rehearsal dinner tomorrow instead of Friday and just incorporate it into the Yule Feast. That's why I wanted to make sure I came out tonight. I won't be home for a few days."

"The wedding is Saturday. What will you do Friday night?"

I smiled. "Friday night is the bachelorette party. Just a mild one. Serena put her foot down on any of us being hungover for her wedding."

Dad chuckled. *"I can understand that. Tell me, have you seen your mother's dress?"*

"I have. It's a lovely midnight blue with silver beadwork. It goes all the way to the ground, and it has a scalloped off-the-shoulder neckline. She looks amazing in it."

"Your mother always looks amazing. Still the most beautiful woman I ever saw in all my millennia." He chuckled. *"Except for you, of course. You look so much like your mother. It both hurts and warms my heart."*

10

"My girl sure can make a mean lasagna," Alex said as he finished drying the plate he had in his hand.

"You realize I could have used a little magic to wash and dry these dishes, right? We could be snuggled next to the fireplace in the library right now with a glass of red wine."

Alex laughed, set the plate inside the cabinet, then leaned down to kiss me. "Doing dishes together builds intimacy and gives us time to connect."

I grinned. "That's such a girl thing to say."

Alex narrowed his eyes. "Psychology 101, Princess. Everyone knows that."

"Is that right?" I bit my lip to keep from laughing. "My apologies, Sheriff."

Alex grabbed hold of both ends of his dish towel and wound it rapidly in the air. "Are you being facetious?"

I threw back my head and laughed. "Yes, I am. And you better not pop me with that towel if you know what's good for you."

"Hmm," Alex said as he took a step toward me. "And just what would you do if I did?"

Using my magic, I turned on the water and lifted the dish sprayer in the air until it was level with his face.

"That's cheating," he said.

"That's improvising," I countered.

Dropping the towel, Alex lunged for me, and in one swift move, threw me over his shoulder. My concentration broke as I hung down Alex's back, causing the sprayer to drop back into place. Waving my hand in the air, I turned off the water as Alex strode out of the room—but not before he grabbed our wine glasses.

"Are you needing assistance, Princess? Should I stick him full of quills?"

I lifted my head and laughed at Needles' hopeful look.

"I'm fine. In fact, you can probably retire for the rest of the night."

Needles rolled his eyes. *"I never get to do anything fun."*

"I can hear you, Porcupine," Alex said as he strode into the library.

"And I can both see and smell you, Gargoyle."

I let out a burst of laughter.

"Go away, Porcupine," Alex said as he set the glasses on the coffee table in front of the oversized fireplace, then carefully lowered me to the ground.

"Please," I added.

Needles huffed, his wings glowing red. *"I don't get paid enough to deal with his insolence, Princess."*

"You don't get paid at all," I reminded him as I used my magic to throw another log on the fire. "How about this? I'll have Mom make you an extra-large waffle tomorrow for breakfast. That should help ease your hurt."

"It'll do. I'm outta here."

He zipped out the library door and headed toward his favorite spot to sleep—in my old baby cradle upstairs.

"Feel like going over some information?" Alex asked.

"Always."

We snuggled on the sofa facing the fire and sipped wine while we hashed out suspects, alibis, and motives.

"Brody Lightweig's motive," Alex said. "He has a hundred thousand dollar life insurance policy out on Celeste, plus they recently broke up because she refused to put him in her will. We know Brody was at Celeste's house on Monday, which is within the timeline of when the poison was added to her drink."

"Next is Garth Trollson," I said. "His motive is he covets what Celeste has. He wants her yoga studio so he can expand his business. He also admitted to sending Celeste threatening letters. He acted confused about just how many notes there were, but I don't buy that. We need to find out if he knew where Celeste lived, and where he was Sunday and Monday."

"I spoke with Deputy Sparks on my way here. He said Trollson claimed he was at the gym until four on Sunday, then met up with friends to watch a supernatural football game on TV. Monday he was at the gym from eight in the morning until five at night. Said he had lunch delivered."

I growled low in my chest. "That's pretty neat and solid."

Alex took a sip of his wine, then set it back down on the table. "How about Laurel Muser? She's admitted to being angry at Celeste for constantly being rejected for admission to the yoga studio. She told us about the huge rivalry between sirens and muses that has gone on for centuries. While we have no proof she went to Celeste's house, she admitted she knows where Celeste lives, and she's related to Brody. She could find out Celeste's schedule fairly easily from him."

"Laurel claims she never left her house because she was meeting a deadline with her book."

"Weak alibi," Alex said. "The next three suspects are low on my list."

"I'd agree. Chloe, Tabby, and LeeAnn?"

"Yep," Alex said. "Chloe will inherit the studio, which gives her a motive, but there doesn't seem to be any stress in their relationship. Chloe hasn't left her side, and she seems happy with the arrangement she has with her sister with regard to working at the studio."

"And I don't see a motive for Tabby, either. I mean, they live together and Tabby has the easiest access to the powder drink, but what's her motive? She gains nothing upon Celeste's death."

"Agree. The same with LeeAnn. What's her motive? She has a key to the room where Celeste makes her drink, but none of the other jars in the room had the water hemlock in them. What does she gain by killing Celeste?"

I picked up my wineglass and took a healthy drink. "I think we agree Brody Lightweig, Garth Trollson, and Laurel Muser are our top suspects." I set my drink on the table and snuggled up next to Alex's side. "I can't wait for Serena and Grant to get back from their honeymoon. I'm so ready for a vacation."

"Me too. It was nice of your mom to offer to watch Zoie. I didn't even have to ask Serena and Grant. I'm picking up my tux before the rehearsal dinner tomorrow night. Then that's about all I need to do until the bachelor party. I told Dash I'd get Grant to the bar on time."

"Isn't that the best man's job?"

"Dash said he wanted to make sure everything was ready at the bar, so I agreed to pick up Grant."

I chuckled. "Sounds like Dash is going all out. Needles and I are having breakfast at Mom's tomorrow morning around nine if you want to eat with us. Then I'm going to leave my vehicle there overnight. It's Yule tomorrow, so after the rehearsal and dinner, I'll stay at Mom's and celebrate with her and GiGi. Actually, I'm staying there the following night as well. Mom's the designated driver for Serena's bachelorette party."

"Zoie and I are going to open one gift around ten for Yule tomorrow night. Maybe if you're still up and feel like getting out, you can come by? It's only a five-minute drive from your mom's."

"Maybe I will." I wrapped my arms around his neck. "Should I bring Needles?"

Alex grinned and pulled me onto his lap. "Only if you want me to stop kissing you."

"Too bad for Needles."

Alex laughed as his lips captured mine, and I forgot about everything else.

11

"**B**reakfast was amazing, Serenity." Alex placed his napkin next to his plate. "Nothing better than Belgian waffles and bacon."

Needles burped and patted his stomach. *"You aren't lying, Gargoyle. You'd think that peanut butter would make me energetic, but I seem to need a nap right now."*

I snorted. "That's because you counteracted the peanut butter when you slathered on all the maple syrup."

Needles—propped up against the syrup bottle—didn't bother answering me. He was already snoring.

"Just leave him here," Mom said. "You can stop by and get him later. I'm meeting Starla, Serena, Tamara, and Grant around noon at Starla's place to finish with the wedding favors."

"I feel awful that I'm not helping out more," I said. "But I think I'm needed here with Alex to find out who tried to poison Celeste." I sighed. "I hope Serena understands."

"Of course she does," Mom said. "In fact, I'd argue she'd kick you out if you tried to help with wedding favors today

59

instead of investigating with Alex." She patted my shoulder. "Just be sure you and Alex get to The Spellmoore by four so we can have the wedding rehearsal. Then immediately afterward, we'll eat at The Spellmoore restaurant, and then you, me, Starla, Serena, and GiGi will celebrate Yule and the Winter Solstice later tonight back here."

"Sounds good. We'll be back to pick up Needles after we go by Brody's place."

Alex and I got into his Blazer and drove to the side of town where Brody lived. Since it was Yule, nearly every store on the island was closed, which meant Brody should be home.

"Now what?" Brody demanded as he opened his front door. "I haven't done anything. After work last night, I went to Wickedly Rome for some Italian food, then came home and went to bed."

Alex smiled. "Thank you, but that's not why we're here. Agent Loci and I just have a few follow-up questions. You can imagine our surprise yesterday when Laurel Muser mentioned she was your—I believe it was second or third cousin?"

"Something like that," Brody said. "We don't exactly run in the same circles. My great-great-grandmother was half muse. That's all. I'm a practicing witch, as you know." He snorted. "Muses usually keep to themselves. They think they're superior to all other supernaturals."

"Where were you Sunday and Monday afternoons?" I asked.

Brody took an involuntary step backward. "Why? Why do you need to know?"

"Again, just asking follow-up questions," Alex said.

"I'm not sure. I guess I was at my restaurant both days."

"What time on Sunday?" I asked.

"Maybe eleven to four. Then I went home. Same for Monday."

"Really?" I said. "And if we have a witness who states they saw you snooping around Celeste's place on Monday afternoon, what would you say?"

Brody cleared his throat. "Oh, that's right. I think I did go by. I wanted to pick up some of my things I'd left over there. But she wasn't home."

"She wasn't home?" I asked. "Or Tabby came home and surprised you and you ran?"

"I didn't do anything!" He sighed. "Look, I wanted to explain about Sonja. Sonja came into the restaurant Sunday afternoon, and then, like ten minutes after she leaves, I'm getting these angry texts from Celeste. I knew Celeste was angry and wouldn't see me, so I thought I'd give her a chance to cool off. I went to see her Monday, only she wasn't home. I was going to leave her a note, but then Tabby came home, and I got scared."

"Who's Sonja?" Alex asked.

"I don't think I should say anything more without a lawyer. If you want to question me further, then it'll be with a lawyer."

He shut the door in our faces, and I was momentarily stunned.

"We obviously hit a nerve," I said.

"Exactly what I was thinking." Alex turned and started back toward his vehicle. "Do you know who Sonja is?"

I shook my head and hopped up inside the Blazer. "No. Not off the top of my head."

My cell phone rang, and I put it on speakerphone. "Hey, Serena. What's up? You guys getting an early start on the wedding favors?"

"Not yet. I just got a call from Tabby and Chloe both. They said Celeste is awake and needs to talk to you. She may have a new lead."

My cell phone dinged, letting me know I had an incoming text. I pulled it up and quickly scanned the message.

"Hey, Serena, that's Chloe now. She just texted Celeste needs to speak to me. Alex and I are on our way to the hospital now."

"I hope you figure this out soon," Serena said. "See you at four for the wedding rehearsal."

"Wouldn't miss it." I hung up the phone and grinned. "Maybe Celeste will know who this Sonja person is."

* * *

"You're looking a thousand times better than the last time I laid eyes on you," I said. "How're you feeling?"

"A thousand times better," Celeste joked. "The witches assigned to me almost have me back to one hundred percent. And look at this room? These lovely plants and spa music. It's like they knew me and tailored the room to me."

Tabby patted Celeste's hand. "It's all part of the magic that makes up this hospital. It adapts to what you need."

"So amazing," Celeste said. "I've honestly never had a reason to come here. Most of my ailments can be treated by the apothecary. I told Chloe we need to make sure we donate the next time the hospital has a fundraiser." Tears filled her eyes. "Thank you for what you did for me, Shayla."

"It was Needles," I said. "He knew the poison was water hemlock."

Celeste wiped a tear from her cheek. "I'll be sure to thank him next time I see him."

Chloe moved from the window to stand next to Celeste's bed. "I want to say before Celeste tells you who might have wanted to hurt her, that I didn't know. She never said anything to me."

"Me, neither," Tabby said, frowning down at Celeste. "If she had, I'd have—"

"You'd have taken matters into your own hands and gotten into trouble," Celeste said. "I didn't want to say anything because I was embarrassed."

"What's going on?" I asked. "What didn't you tell anyone?"

Celeste sighed. "I think Brody was seeing Sonja Birdly, another siren."

"Not just another siren," Tabby said, "but your rival. This girl has it out for you because you're getting work, and she can't handle that."

Alex put up his hand. "What kind of work?"

"Singing," Celeste said. "I've never put myself out there like other sirens do. My love has always been yoga. Opening the studio was my dream for—I don't know? Forever?"

Tabby and Chloe both laughed and nodded their heads.

"So when the Earthly sisters asked me to sing at their wedding because it was Samhain and Sonja was already booked at a local bar, I said yes. That's where Serena heard me and asked me to sing at her wedding. And she wasn't the only one who approached me. I had other bar owners contact me as well." Celeste sighed and glanced down at her blanket. "I told the bar owners no, but said yes to Serena. I mean, it's like the most exciting thing to happen on the island in a long time. I was honored."

"You don't have to make excuses for why you said yes," Tabby said. "You *should* be honored."

Celeste smiled. "I know. Well, when Sonja found out I was singing at Serena's wedding, she started hounding me. Calling me, threatening me without really threatening me. Then, about three weeks ago, she told me she'd hurt me in a way I wouldn't recover. I thought she meant physically, so I was diligent about not being alone if I could help it."

"Did you tell anyone?" I asked. "Brody?"

Tears filled Celeste's eyes again. "I finally told Brody right before—right before we broke up. When I first told him, he was really mad. He said he'd take care of it. But then I found out what Brody had done, and I..." Her voice trailed off and she looked away.

"Found out what?" Tabby and Chloe demanded simultaneously.

"Why did you call off the wedding?" Chloe added. "Because of the will? Or was there more to it?"

"I found out Brody had taken out a life insurance policy on me." Celeste looked at her sister and then Tabby. "A hundred thousand dollar life insurance policy."

Both girls gasped.

"Well, if that isn't motive, I don't know what is!" Chloe exclaimed. "You should be able to arrest him now."

"We spoke to Mr. Highwolf yesterday," Alex said. "And we've also spoken to Brody about it. I can't divulge anything more at this point. I hope you understand." He glanced down at Celeste. "Tell me more about Brody and Sonja. You think Sonja is another suspect we need to look at?"

Celeste shrugged. "I thought maybe. See, on Sunday afternoon, I received some texts and pictures." She grabbed her cell phone off the tray next to her bed, scrolled, then handed the phone to me. "You can't see Sonja very well, but that's Brody resting on her shoulder. Scroll over a couple more pictures, and I have selfie snaps of them kissing, taken by Sonja."

I scrolled and handed the phone to Alex. There was something vaguely familiar about the woman's hair, but I couldn't place where I'd seen it before.

"I guess she finally did hurt me," Celeste said.

Chloe snorted. "That idiot was never good enough for you."

Celeste let out a watery laugh. "You're my sister. You're supposed to say that."

Tabby growled. "You know I never liked him."

"I just don't know how Sonja would have gotten inside our house," Celeste said. "How could she have put the poison in my jar?"

"That's what we're trying to narrow down," I said. "We believe the poison was added at your house either on Sunday or Monday. Can you tell us where you were on both those days?"

"At my studio," Celeste said. "I have a ten o'clock class and a one o'clock class both days. In between, I'll work in my shop in the back. I think I got out of my one o'clock yoga class around two-thirty on Sunday and then worked on soaps and body scrub until four. Sunday nights are always family nights, which means I have dinner with Chloe and her husband and kids. I usually get home around seven or eight at the latest. On Monday, I think I got home around five."

"And you, Tabby?" I asked.

"I worked Sunday from two to midnight. Celeste was already in bed when I got home Sunday night. I didn't work Monday, but like I told you before, I did run some errands in the afternoon."

"Thank you for this information," I said. "We'll be sure and speak with Sonja Birdly today."

"I guess I'll see you tonight then," Celeste said.

"What?" I mused. "You're getting sprung from here?"

Celeste laughed. "I am. And I'm definitely making it to the rehearsal tonight."

"Can't wait," I said.

Alex and I said goodbye, exited the room, and rode the

elevator in silence. We didn't say anything until we got back inside the Blazer and Alex pulled up Sonja Birdly's address.

"I'd say the best time for someone to break into Celeste's house would be Sunday," I said. "That's the biggest window."

"And you heard Celeste say Sunday nights were family nights. I'd say that's something her fiancé would know, wouldn't you?"

"Yep." As we exited the parking lot, I settled back in my seat. "I'd bet anything he knew Celeste wouldn't be home, and just maybe he told his new girlfriend the same thing."

Alex smiled. "I'm counting on it."

"Let's stop and pick up Needles at Mom's before we go see Sonja."

❧ 12 ❧

Sonja Birdly lived two miles outside town in a small housing development. Alex parked in her driveway, and we hurried up the sidewalk. Flurries had once again started to fall.

"The older I get," Needles said from inside my backpack, *"the more I think I should retire to a tropical island."*

"I'm for that," Alex said. "In fact, I'll help you pack."

"Ha ha, Gargoyle. You aren't getting rid of me that easily."

Ignoring the two, I knocked on Sonja's door. A few seconds later, the door opened, and I barely suppressed a gasp. Now I knew why the hair seemed so familiar.

"You're the secretary who works for Leo Highwolf," I said. "Now it's starting to make sense."

"Can I help you?" Sonja asked.

"We'd like to come in and ask you some questions," Alex said.

After a moment's hesitation, Sonja finally stepped back and motioned us inside. "I just put on some tea to help my lunch digest. Let's go into the kitchen." She looked Needles up and down. "Birds, dragons, insects…those are supposed to fly in the sky. Porcupines are not included on that list."

"How about I save us time and just cut out her tongue now?"

"His name is Needles, and I'd appreciate it if you didn't insult my partner and friend," I said. "It pisses me off, and when I get pissed, I usually solve it by hitting something. Hard."

Alex chuckled.

Sonja huffed. "Did you just threaten me?"

I shrugged. "I don't know? Did I?"

"How about we go to the kitchen?" Alex said, sending me a wink.

The inside of Sonja Birdly's house was decorated in birds. Bird wallpaper, bird upholstery, bird photographs…and that was just in the living room. There were bird dishes and decanters in the kitchen, so I didn't even blink an eye when she handed Alex and me hot tea in bird teacups.

"This is all a little creepy," Needles hissed from my shoulder. *"I feel like the birds are plotting against me."*

"We should be so lucky," Alex murmured as Sonja retrieved her cup from off the counter.

"I know about Celeste in the hospital," Sonja said as she sat down across from us, "but I had nothing to do with it."

"We've spoken to both Brody and Celeste," I said. "We know you have been threatening to hurt Celeste if she didn't stop taking singing jobs around the island. We also saw the photos you texted her Sunday where you are kissing Brody."

"And?" She took a sip of her tea. "My threats were never about physically harming her, they were about hurting her where it counts…in her heart. After all, she's hurting me in my heart every time she takes away a music job I want."

I frowned. "The only 'job' Celeste may have taken was Serena's wedding, and that was never yours, anyway."

"Isn't that enough?" Sonja asked, her voice going up an octave. "This wedding is a huge deal. This should have been mine! I'm the wedding singer on the island. There are sirens who perform locally at bars and whatnot, but *I'm* the siren who sings at weddings. Not Celeste. She hasn't put in the time and effort like I have."

"Entitlement doesn't really make for a good alibi," Alex said. "In fact, it makes for a good motive."

I bit the inside of my cheek to keep from smiling. He was spot on with that observation. Sonja's face and neck turned red, but she didn't say anything. Since he'd already managed to get under her skin, I let Alex take the lead.

"So what did you do?" Alex mused. "Call Celeste and tell her Brody took out a life insurance policy on her?"

"I simply called and asked for further information regarding the one hundred thousand dollar life insurance policy Mr. High-wolf was working on," Sonja said. "I had no idea Celeste didn't know."

One corner of Alex's mouth lifted. "Nice. You almost said that with a straight face."

Sonja shrugged. "It would be hard for you to prove otherwise."

I frowned. "When did you take those pictures you sent Celeste Sunday?"

"Brody and I were together Saturday night."

"Tell us about that," Alex said.

"He came into Ghostly Pub where I was singing. One thing led to another, and by the time I finished my set around ten that night, he was sauced. I sat with him, gave him some more to drink, listened to him go on and on about his new plan being ruined, and how he should have stuck to the original plan." She smiled. "He was sure Leo had called Celeste and told her about

69

the life insurance policy, but it was me. So I took advantage of the situation. I gave him another drink, came on to him, took some photos, and sent them to that little job stealer the next day."

"This plan Brody mentioned," Alex said. "Why don't you tell us about this original plan of his?"

Sonja shrugged. "I don't know. He was drunk, so I figured it was just drunk rambling. I will tell you, I got the impression he wasn't as heartbroken about the relationship as Celeste. He was more angry." She shrugged. "But I have no idea what this original plan of his was."

Needles snorted. *"I do. To get Celeste to fall in love with him, and then kill her so he could collect the insurance."*

"Where were you Sunday and Monday?" I asked.

"All day?" Sonja asked.

I gave her a tight smile. "All day. Both days."

"I woke up late on Sunday thanks to the drinking Saturday night. I had some food, practiced my singing, then went to town to Brody's taco restaurant to see how he was feeling." Sonja laughed. "That idiot had no idea who I was. He didn't even remember talking to me Saturday. That's why I sent those pictures to Celeste on Sunday. I wanted her to hurt. How dare he just dismiss me! After I left the restaurant, I sent the pictures, went home, watched a couple programs I had on my DVR, then went to bed."

"And Monday?" Alex asked.

"I was at work from nine to five," Sonja said. "After work, I grabbed a bite to eat at the bar I was singing in, went on stage from seven to ten, then went home."

"Do you know where Celeste lives?" I asked.

"I guess. I mean, I'm sure we have it on file at the office. Plus, I'm sure I know someone who knows where she lives. Why? You think I went to her house in the middle of the night and poisoned her somehow?" Sonja snorted. "I can assure you I didn't."

"Thank you for your time," Alex said. "We'll let you get back to your day."

"In case you're thinking of calling my boss and tattling on me about calling Celeste, he already knows. After you guys left, he called me in to ask me if I ever contacted Celeste. I feigned ignorance and played it off like it was a misunderstanding." She gave us a tight smile. "He believed me."

"I hope she's the bad guy so I can rough her up when we take her down," Needles said as we walked toward Alex's vehicle. *"Imagine telling me it was unnatural for me to fly! The nerve of that little twit!"*

I laughed and closed the Blazer's door. "I didn't like her either, but I'm not sure if she's behind the poisoning. Except for the movie watching Sunday night, it was a pretty solid alibi. But we know Celeste was home Sunday night by seven, so I don't know if that gives Sonja enough time to enter Celeste's house." I turned to Alex. "We need more information about these plans Brody had. Are we going to arrest him? Or at least take him in?"

Alex sighed. "It's going on two. If we go out and arrest Brody, and he yells for an attorney like he already said he would, maybe he gets one on Yule, maybe he doesn't—it's going to be four of five before all that gets settled. Then we'd have to question him. I don't want to mess up Serena and Grant's big night. Brody manages a restaurant in town, he has family on the island…he's not going to flee. We can wait until tomorrow to haul him down to the station."

I smiled. "I was hoping you'd say that."

13

The rehearsal and Yule dinner went off without a hitch. Having Celeste present made it even more special. I kissed Alex goodbye next to The Spellmoore fountain out front with a promise to see him later that evening.

"I saw Zoie's gift on your mom's counter," Needles said as he settled down in the back of Mom's car. *"She's going to love it."*

"I hope she does," I said. "Every witch needs her own cauldron. Mom and GiGi got her some candles and a couple crystals."

Mom slid behind the wheel of her car, turned over the engine, and pulled out of the resort's parking lot. "I can't wait to get out of this dress and into something more comfortable."

"What time are Serena, Aunt Starla, and GiGi coming over?" I asked.

"After they change clothes at Starla's," Mom said. "I'm glad GiGi is staying in town until after the wedding."

I grinned. "She's talked nonstop about the bachelorette party tomorrow night. I think GiGi plans on getting her groove on."

Mom groaned. "Please don't ever say those words aloud again."

Needles laughed from the back.

"I checked the weather for Saturday," I said. "We may get snow during the wedding."

"That'll be pretty," Mom said. "We are so blessed to be witches. Not many people can have an outdoor wedding in the snow and not feel a single flake."

"Thanks to your magic. You're sure you can hold the shield for that many hours? Through both the wedding and reception?"

Mom patted my knee. "I've got it. Don't you worry. Plus, a couple other witches offered to help as well."

We drove the rest of the way home in silence. I thought about the case and the arrest we were about to make in the morning. I wasn't sure if the proof was enough I could call in my ex-partner, Zane, from the Paranormal Apprehension and Detention Agency to take Brody away, or if Brody would have to be prosecuted through the supernatural courts. Zane was called for supernaturals caught red-handed committing violent acts or murder. We really just had a bunch of circumstantial evidence against Brody, but it was enough for attempted murder.

By the time we arrived back at Mom's, I had my second wind. Serena, Aunt Starla, and GiGi came over and we celebrated Yule by making wreaths and eating a ton of leftover desserts from Serena's reject wedding pile.

"What time are you meeting up with Grant tonight?" I asked Serena as the two of us finished drying dishes.

"I'm not. We're trying to not be alone with each other until the day of the wedding."

"Seriously?" I placed the stack of china plates in Mom's hutch. "That's commendable."

Serena snorted. "It was Mom's idea."

Needles let out a loud snore from his position on the counter.

"That porcupine can sleep anywhere," Serena joked.

"Listen, I'm not meeting Alex until around ten. Mom, Aunt Starla, and GiGi took a bottle of wine with them into the living room, so we won't be seeing them until the morning. I'd like to do a little stakeout tonight."

I quickly filled her in on the arrest we were about to make in the morning, and why we were waiting.

"Not that I expect anything to go wrong tonight," I said. "But I'd like to at least look in on Brody."

"You guys shouldn't have worried about messing up our rehearsal and Yule celebration. I'm sure everyone would have understood why you—no, never mind." Serena let out a little laugh. "You'd never have heard the end of it from GiGi, my mom, or your mom. You made the right choice."

I grinned. "So you want to ride with me?"

"You bet!"

I sneaked into the living room to make sure everyone was still drinking wine and reminiscing about Yules past, then Serena and I jumped inside my Bronco and headed over to Brody's place.

The island was aglow with all the Christmas lights and decorations. Even Brody's place was lit up when I parked across the street from his house.

"We'll just stay an hour or so." I turned off the headlights but left the vehicle running for the heat. "I just want to make sure nothing goes wrong."

We'd been sitting across from Brody's house for about twenty minutes, watching the flicker of a TV in his front room, when a tap on Serena's window caused us both to scream.

Alex and Grant grinned at us through the window.

"I see we all have the same idea," Alex said, as Serena

hopped out of the Bronco and pushed the seat forward so the guys could get into the back. "At some point, Shayla, you may have to look into getting a vehicle with four doors."

I laughed. "Never."

"No Needles?" Grant asked.

"Left him sleeping at Mom's," I said.

"Anything good going on?" Alex asked.

"Nothing yet," Serena said. "But it's still early."

No sooner had Serena said those words than a vehicle turned onto Brody's street. We all scrunched down lower in our seats so we wouldn't be seen. The vehicle turned and parked in Brody's driveway.

"Look who it is," I said. "Sonja Birdly."

"And look what she's wearing," Alex said. "A black coat with white fur around the hood."

"The same one Tamara has," Serena said. "Is that important?"

"It would be," I said, "if we didn't already know that about forty women on this island have the same coat. But a witness said they saw a lady in a black coat with white fur looking inside Celeste's windows Sunday."

Brody's front door opened, and Sonja stepped inside.

"Does Sonja being here prove anything?" Serena asked.

"I don't think it *proves* anything," I said, "but it definitely goes toward motive. Get rid of Celeste, and the two of them can be together."

Alex leaned forward from the back and stuck his head near my shoulder. "Sonja told us Brody didn't remember who she was Sunday afternoon when she went to see him at the restaurant. Obviously, that was a lie to throw us off track."

"But why not just break off the engagement?" Serena asked. "If Brody was seeing Sonja secretly, why not just break up?"

75

"The life insurance policy," Alex said. "Brody goes ahead with the marriage, and shortly thereafter, Celeste dies."

"With Celeste dead," Grant piped up, "Brody and Sonja would have a nice little nest egg."

I nodded in agreement. "But I can't believe Brody is so dense that he never suspected Sonja was the one to call Celeste and tell her of the policy. It's unbelievable."

"Yeah," Alex said, "that one still confuses me."

Brody's front door opened, and Sonja stormed outside.

"That didn't take long," Serena said.

"She looks pissed," I added.

Brody appeared in the doorway and pointed a finger at Sonja.

"Of all the times to leave Needles at home," I said. "He could eavesdrop for us."

Sonja marched over to Brody and slapped him across the face.

Alex chuckled. "Or maybe Needles isn't needed. I think we got the gist."

Sonja stomped over to her car, got inside, and sped away as Brody went back inside his house.

"What was that all about?" I asked. "Did Brody just call it off between them?"

"But why?" Serena asked.

I shrugged. "Because Celeste is feeling better, and he's hoping to get back together?"

Alex grunted. "More like he's afraid we're getting close, and he's trying to distance himself from Sonja."

"I think that's more plausible," Grant said.

I sighed. "Well, now what? Do we still wait until tomorrow to arrest Brody?"

"Yes." Alex leaned up from the back and kissed my cheek. "It's almost nine. You're due at my house in an hour to celebrate with Zoie and me. When I left the house to pick up Grant, she was pulling cookies out of the oven."

"Before I forget," I said, "Mom wanted me to tell you she's having a big breakfast at her house in the morning. You and Zoie are invited."

"Same goes for you," Serena said to Grant. "Walt is coming too."

Walt Hawkins, former Sheriff of Enchanted Island, was also walking Serena down the aisle. Walt and Serena's dad had been best friends in school, and after Serena's dad had disappeared at sea, Walt helped raise Serena, even though Aunt Starla had never married him.

Serena hopped out of the vehicle to let the guys out of the backseat. "This was fun. See you both in the morning."

"And I'll see you and Zoie in an hour," I said to Alex.

❦ 14 ❦

"I love my cauldron," Zoie said the next morning as she put the bottle of maple syrup back in the pantry. "And the candles and crystals. You guys shouldn't have gone so crazy."

"Nonsense." GiGi sipped her coffee and popped a piece of leftover bacon in her mouth. She'd gotten out of helping Zoie, Serena, and me clean the kitchen after breakfast by complaining her bones were aching and they needed to rest up for the bachelorette party later. "That's what Yule is for. And every witch needs her own cauldron."

"What do you still have to do at The Spellmoore?" I asked Serena.

"Deliver the last of the wedding favors, meet one last time with the staff catering the meal, and then Tamara and I are going back to the bakery to decorate my wedding cake."

I let out a little squeal of excitement and gave Serena a hug. "I can't believe you're getting married tomorrow!"

GiGi cackled. "I can't believe I'm gonna be drinking and getting my boogie on in about ten hours."

78

Serena narrowed her eyes at GiGi. "Absolutely no one, including you, is going to be hungover for my wedding."

GiGi rolled her eyes. "The wedding isn't until four in the afternoon. I'll have had a good amount of hours to recover by then. Throw on a little glamour magic, and I'll be looking so good I'll be breaking hearts."

"Speaking of breaking hearts, GiGi," I said. "Did you invite Byron Sealy to the wedding?"

"You hush your mouth right now," GiGi snapped. "I ain't dating that old selkie. He couldn't handle a witchy woman like me."

"But I bet he'd like to try!" I exclaimed, then ducked when GiGi waved her hand and sent a slice of leftover French toast covered in powdered sugar my way.

"What the—"

Alex broke off as the toast hit him square in the face... causing us all to burst out laughing.

He yanked the toast off his face, leaving behind a coating of powdered sugar on his lips and cheeks. Tossing the toast in the trash, he turned to look at me. "I was coming in to see if you were ready to arrest Brody?"

"I'm ready." I handed him a wet washcloth. "I just need to put on my service belt and say bye to Mom."

"We're gonna have strippers tonight," I heard GiGi say as I headed out of the kitchen. "You gonna have strippers at your party, Sheriff?"

I heard Alex sputtering and the girls all laughing, so I headed upstairs as fast as I could to retrieve my belt and wake up Needles from his sugar-high nap. I cared about Alex too much to leave him down there alone.

* * *

E verything looked just like it had last night when Alex parked next to Brody's car. Even his Christmas lights were still on.

"At some point today," Needles said as he flew out the passenger-side door, *"I'm going to need a nap. I'm too old to stay up all day and all night."*

Alex met my eyes over the hood of his vehicle. "I still don't understand why Needles has to go with me to the bachelor party. He's *your* bodyguard. He should be with you."

"Get real, Gargoyle. Besides, this is the first time I've actively participated in such debauchery. And I can't wait. Will there be sword fighting? Or mead drinking? Because I'm quite adept at both those things."

I let out a bark of laughter as I knocked on Brody's door. After a few minutes, when no one answered, I knocked again.

Alex pulled out his cell phone. "I'll call Howling Good Tacos & Nachos and see what time he's working today."

I raised an eyebrow at Needles.

Needles sighed dramatically and did a twirl in the air, his wings glowing deep purple. *"Or I can just go down the chimney and take a look around."*

Alex crossed his arms over his chest. "That's not exactly legal."

Sometimes it was hard to remember I no longer worked for the Paranormal Apprehension and Detention Agency. When I did work for them, police work was a lot easier. In some ways, my old partner and I were more like government-issued bounty hunters. If we were chasing down a supernatural bad guy, we didn't really worry about warrants and trespassing and things like that. We had a job to do, and we did it however we had to. But that was how the government allowed us to work. It wasn't quite the same with supernatural police work.

"What's the worst that can happen?" I mused. "He catches Brody in the shower?"

Needles covered his eyes with his paws. *"My eyes! My eyes! Forget it. I've changed my mind. Call the restaurant."*

Alex and I both laughed.

I didn't say it aloud, but I sort of liked the fact that Alex could now hear Needles. It could sometimes get awkward when it was just Needles and me bantering back and forth. And then I'd have to explain it to Alex. But now it was like he was in on the joke.

Needles took off toward the top of the roof, gave us a salute, then nosedived down the chimney.

"He's not exactly subtle, is he?" Alex asked dryly.

I laughed. "I don't think Needles knows what the word even means."

A few seconds later, Needles burst out of the chimney, his red wings working double time.

"It's Brody! He's dead!"

❧ 15 ❧

Alex nudged me aside, shifted into a gargoyle, and rammed the front door open. Shifting back to human, he turned to me. "Before we call Doc and Finn to the scene, let's make sure he's dead and not just passed out. Maybe he celebrated a little too hard last night after Sonja left."

"*I know dead, Gargoyle,*" Needles sneered.

"I'm sure you do," Alex said as he stepped farther inside Brody's house. "But we need to go by the book."

"If he *is* dead, we know the timeline is between nine last night and nine this morning," I said as I walked around the sofa. "Oh, boy."

Lying on the floor in a fetal position was Brody Lightweig… an overturned decanter on the coffee table and evidence of a broken glass next to him.

"I have dried blood on his temple," Alex said. "Plus signs of Brody's head hitting the edge of the coffee table."

"Did he fall, hit his head, and die?" I mused.

"Perhaps. He could also have been poisoned, tried to stand, fell and hit his head."

"I'll bag the decanter and broken glass for Finn." Using my magic, I conjured up two evidence bags, levitated the items into the bags, then stepped away so Alex could examine Brody closer.

"No pulse," he said.

"I'll call Doc and Finn now. We're only about three miles from the station, so it shouldn't take them long to get here."

Alex cursed under his breath. "I told Opal and Pearl with it being the holidays and a Friday, if we had nothing pressing, they could clock out early and just have Officer Sparks run his shift from two to seven. They're gonna skin me alive if they have to stay late today."

I put a call into Pearl so she could send Doc and Finn our way. Next, I called Opal upstairs at the sheriff's station so she'd know what we were dealing with. As I spoke to Opal, I crossed over to the end table next to the sofa and frowned down at the printed note. Disconnecting the phone, I levitated the letter.

"Got a typed note left here," I said.

"What's it say?" Alex asked.

"It says, 'I'm sorry for all the hurt I caused. I should have stuck to my original plan to have Celeste fall in love with me, and then stand her up at the altar. Instead, I became greedy and took out the life insurance policy on her. I went to her house Monday, used the key hidden under the rock in the backyard, and put the poison in her vitamin drink that was sitting out in the kitchen. My plan was to collect on the insurance. I'm sorry for what I've done. I hope everyone can forgive me.' It's signed Brody."

"Did he sign it in his own hand?" Alex asked. "Or is it a typed signature?"

"It's all typed," I said. "I'll bag it, and then check out the back rooms and bag the computer and printer so Gordon can check it out."

"Good idea."

I started down the hallway, then turned and greeted Doc and Finn when they hurried inside the house.

"I can't believe this," Finn said. "Brody is dead? This is going to devastate his mother. Brody was an only child, and his dad left the island when Brody was only five. It's always just been the two of them."

"And over the holidays," Doc added. "While bad news is never good, it's especially hard around this time."

"Let's get to work," Alex said. "Brody's mom deserves to know what happened here."

"I have a suicide note, decanter, and a broken glass already in evidence bags," I said. "I'm going to bag the computer and printer now for Gordon."

"I'll get on them immediately," Finn said. "It shouldn't take me long to run an analysis on the contents in the glass. Especially since I know what to look for."

I glanced over at Alex. "You're thinking we'll find water hemlock in the decanter?"

"I'd say so," Alex said.

"Can you give me until two for the autopsy results?" Doc mused.

Alex nodded. "I can do that. Finn, would you mind photographing the scene for me?"

I hurried down the hallway and peeked inside the open doorways until I found the office room. Once again, I conjured up two large evidence bags.

Needles hovered near the door. *You think Brody took his own life because he knew we were on to him?*

I shrugged. "Maybe. We'll know more when Doc finishes the autopsy." I waved my hands and the two electronics floated toward the door. "I'm going to put these in Finn's vehicle. Then we can go see if Alex needs any more help processing the scene."

Once I magically deposited the electronics in the back of Finn's vehicle, I shut the trunk and noticed some of Brody's neighbors were on their lawns whispering to each other. I knew how quickly gossip could spread, so I hurried inside to get Alex.

"Are we about done?" I asked.

"Just about," Alex said. "Why?"

"We got nosy neighbors," I said. "We need to tell Brody's mom what's happened before someone calls her to ask what's going on over here."

Alex stood. "You're right. Normally I'd have Grant or Officer Sparks notify next-of-kin, but we can't do that today."

"I'll put a ward on the house," I said. "This way, no one can enter after Finn and Doc leave."

"I'll take the rest of the evidence bags with me when I leave," Finn said. "You two be careful."

Needles, Alex, and I exited Brody's house and got inside the Blazer. While Alex pulled up Ms. Lightweig's address, I thought about the fight we saw last night with Sonja.

"Do you think Sonja poisoned Brody?" I asked.

"Maybe," Alex said as he pulled out of the driveway. "Not sure if we've found any evidence that would prove that, though."

"After we let Ms. Lightweig know what's happened," I said, "we should tell Celeste."

"I'd also like to speak to Sonja and Laurel as well."

"Why don't you drop me off at Serenity's place. You can handle all this without me. I need my beauty sleep so I can party all night.

"It'll have to be quick," I said. "We need to get to Ms. Light-weig before the citizens of Enchanted Island get to her."

"Just slow down enough so I can fly out the window."

❧ 16 ❧

As luck would have it, Ms. Lightweig lived on the west side of town, so we had to drive by Mom's to get there. We dropped off Needles, then pulled into Ms. Lightweig's driveway a few minutes later.

"I hate doing this," Alex said. "Worst part of the job."

"This wasn't something I normally did, either. When working for PADA, Zane and I just captured the bad guys and escorted them to the prison, where they were stripped of their supernatural powers. We never had to do notifications like this. If there was a dead body, the local paranormal police would do the calling."

The two pine trees in Ms. Lightweig's yard were decorated with dried fruits and berries...a sure sign she'd celebrated Yule last night.

"Is she a member of your coven or a different one?" Alex asked.

"Neither. She's a solitary witch. I know a couple divorced witches have tried to get a coven together on the island, but nothing ever came of it. We also have a need for a widow and widower coven as well, but no one has risen to that challenge, either."

Alex knocked on the front door of Ms. Lightweig's house. A few seconds later, the front door opened, and Ms. Lightweig's hands flew to her mouth as she bent over at the waist, her eyes never leaving Alex's.

"It's true then?" she panted out. "Something has happened to my son? I've received two calls already about police vehicles being at his house." Tears ran down her cheeks. "One of the vehicles was Doc's van."

"Can we come inside, Ms. Lightweig?" Alex asked.

"No! Tell me now!"

Alex took a deep breath. "I'm afraid we found Brody dead this morning in his living room. We're sorry for your loss."

Ms. Lightweig's knees buckled, and Alex reached out and grabbed her before she hit the ground. "How? I don't under-stand." She pushed Alex away and steady herself with the door-frame. "He was fine last night when I spoke to him over the phone."

"Doc Drago is with him now," Alex said. "When we have answers, we'll let you know."

Anger flashed in Ms. Lightweig's eyes, and she pursed her lips. "Was it that siren girl, Celeste? Did she do something to my poor Brody? He loved her so much, and then she just went and broke off the engagement. No reason at all! Have you spoken to her? Did she admit to hurting my son?"

I wisely kept my mouth shut as Ms. Lightweig went on and on about Celeste. It wouldn't do any good to correct Ms. Light-weig's perception of what had truly transpired between Brody and Celeste at this point. She was a grieving mother.

Ms. Lightweig finally let us inside so I could put on some hot tea while Alex sat with her on the couch. Her neighbor, Maize

Woodelf, came over to aid in the comfort. With another promise to let Ms. Lightweig know what had happened to Brody when Doc knew more, we left the house.

"That was hard," I said.

"I didn't think we'd get anything useful from her. That's why I didn't question her. She obviously has no idea what Brody has been doing with regard to the poisoning and life insurance policy, or any idea about this plan of his to hurt Celeste by leaving her at the altar."

"Now where?" I asked.

"I want to tell Celeste what has happened, question Sonja as to why she was at Brody's house last night, and then I'd like to talk to Laurel again and see if she's spoke with her distant cousin in the last day or two."

As I suspected, Celeste took the news of Brody's death hard. Even though he'd broken her heart, and may have tried to poison her *and* kill her, she still grieved for him.

"I hate to even bring this up," Alex said, "but Brody mentioned in the note he left that he should have stuck to the original plan and just left you at the altar and not taken an insurance policy out on you. Do you—"

Celeste gasped. "What? What are you saying? That he never loved me?"

Tabby patted her knee. "Just hear the sheriff out, Celeste."

"Did you have any idea Brody was setting you up for a fall?" Alex mused. "That his feelings for you were never true?"

Celeste shook her head. "No. Never." She turned to Tabby. "Did you?"

Tabby also shook her head. "No. I didn't like him, but not because I thought his feelings weren't genuine."

"Why would he do this to me?" Celeste asked. "I just don't understand."

"Was he in debt?" I asked. "I mean, he took out a hundred thousand dollar insurance policy out on you. Was he hurting for money?"

"Not that I know of. He makes decent money as a manager." Celeste shrugged. "He never said anything to me if he was struggling financially."

"He said in his note he got in by using the key hidden in the backyard," I said. "Is that possible? Did he know about a hidden key?"

Celeste closed her eyes and nodded. "Yes. Which I guess makes sense. I mean, it's not like any windows were broken or anything to alert us to a break-in. He must have used the key."

"Thank you for your time," Alex said as he stood. "And I'm sorry for everything you've gone through."

I hugged Celeste. "You take it easy. Don't overdue anything."

"I won't. I was going to go to the bachelorette party tonight, but now I'm not sure. Maybe I'll just stay home."

"Serena will understand," I said. "You need to take care of you. If I don't see you tonight, I'll see you Saturday at the wedding."

Back inside the Blazer, I buckled my seatbelt and turned to Alex. "Should we get hold of Brody's bank statements?"

Alex shrugged and pulled out of the driveway. "Not sure it really matters now. Debt would be the best guess as to why he took out the insurance policy. If Doc rules this a suicide, then there's no need to look any further as to his real motive for taking out the policy."

Sonja Birdly was in her front yard filling her bird feeder when we pulled up to her house. Frowning, she stood where she was as we headed her way.

"What's going on?" she asked.

"I'm afraid we have some bad news," Alex said. "This morning, Brody Lightweig was found dead in his home."

Sonja gasped and dropped the bag of birdseed. "What? How? Are you sure?"

"At this time, the cause of death isn't certain," Alex said. "Agent Loci and I have a few questions we'd like to ask you."

"About what?" Sonja said, her eyes filling with tears. "I didn't kill him. I stupidly cared for him."

I shifted my stance in the snow. "Is that why you stormed out of his house last night and slapped him?"

"How do you know I—were you spying on us?" Sonja demanded. "Is that even legal?"

I snorted. "It's legal. Now, what was the fight about?"

"It wasn't a fight. Not really. Look, I went over there to talk to Brody about how we'd left things. I was angry that he wasn't returning my calls, and I was a little put out because you guys had questioned me." She crossed her arms over her black jacket with faux white fur. "When I confronted him last night, he told me I was pathetic and that just because he cried on my shoulder didn't mean he was going to date me. He still thought he could win Celeste back. He told me to get lost and not come back. Once again, I'd lost out to Celeste. When he followed me outside, I had this urge to strike out at him and hurt him like he'd hurt me. So I did. I slapped him and left. If you were there, you saw that. You know I left. I didn't return later and kill Brody."

"What did you do when you left his house?" I asked.

"I came home. And, no, I don't have anyone who can corroborate that. But it's the truth."

"Is that a new coat?" I asked.

"What?" Sonja looked down at herself. "This coat? Yes. I got it recently from Betty's Boo-tique. She had this huge winter coat sale."

"Thank you for your time," Alex said. "If we have more questions, we'll contact you."

We got back in the vehicle and headed out to Laurel's place. Snow was softly falling, making the roads wet and slick. It took a little longer than usual to reach Laurel's house.

"Brody's mother called me," Laurel said when she opened her front door clad in lounge pants and an oversized cashmere sweater. "It's tragic. It also wasn't necessary for you to travel all this way in this weather to tell me."

"It was no problem," Alex said. "We're sorry for your loss."

Laurel lifted one shoulder and sighed. "Thank you. I wasn't exactly close to Brody, but he was family. Now, it's rather cold out there. If you don't mind, I'd like to close the door and keep the heat inside."

"Then you don't mind if we come in?" Alex mused.

Laurel frowned. "Why?"

"Just a few follow-up questions," Alex said. "We've learned a few things since we last spoke."

Laurel sighed again and opened the door, motioning us in. "I'm still on deadline. Can we make it quick, please?"

Alex and I stepped inside the expansive foyer, and I breathed in the pine scent permeating throughout the house.

"Were you aware Brody had taken out an insurance policy on Celeste?" Alex asked.

Laurel's eyes widened. "What? No, I wasn't."

"What about his plan to leave Celeste at the altar?" I asked. "Did you know about that?"

Humor danced in Laurel's eyes. "No. But that sounds exactly like something Brody would do. He was kind of a jerk like that." She shrugged. "Personally, I don't know what Celeste saw in him. I mean, I'm no fan of Celeste Morningsong, but even *I* thought she could do better." Laurel tucked a wayward hair behind her ear. "So he was going to leave Celeste heartbroken at the altar, was he?" She smiled. "I guess I can have that small pleasure."

I frowned. "That's a little harsh, don't you think?"

"Not at all," Laurel said. "I told you, Celeste and I are not friends. Now, if that's everything, I really should get back to work."

❧ 17 ❧

"Thanks for the quick bite," I said as I took one last sip of my fountain drink before exiting the vehicle.

"Can't have you partying tonight on an empty stomach." Alex opened the station's door to head downstairs. "And you need to make sure you drink plenty of non-alcoholic fluids."

I grinned. "I have no intention of drinking a ton of booze tonight."

"Uh-huh. Keep telling yourself that."

Pearl smiled when she saw us hit the bottom of the stairs. "Hello, Sheriff. Please tell me you've solved this, and we can leave for the day? I promised my husband this morning I'd be home for a quickie at noon, and I've already had to disappoint him. He can't take much more disappointment at his age, and I'd hate to marry him and bury him all in the same year. Plus, I need to rest up before I shake my booty all night long."

"You and Opal go on home," Alex said. "We shouldn't be much longer."

Pearl snatched up the phone and pressed a button. "Move

94

your butt, Sister. The sheriff says we can go home. Meet out at the car." With a nod to both of us, Pearl popped up out of her seat, grabbed her purse, and shuffled over to the stairs. "See ya tonight, Shayla."

"That is one strange witch," Alex said as Pearl let out a whoop and levitated herself up the stairs.

We headed down the hallway, Alex still shaking his head. He knocked once on Doc's door before we stepped inside.

"It's as we thought," Doc said. "All signs point to poison. There's damage in the mouth, esophagus, and digestive track. No sign of foul play on or in the body."

"And I found traces of water hemlock in the decanter," Finn said. "Interestingly, though, the amount of water hemlock was triple the amount that was in Celeste's jar."

"Why do you suppose that is?" I mused.

"Maybe Brody wanted Celeste to suffer," Alex said. "By ingesting small doses, it made her sick over the last few days, thereby prolonging her death."

I snorted. "So he takes the easy way out by making sure he triples his dosage, killing him instantly?" I rolled my eyes. "What a piece of work he was."

"With the amount found in the decanter," Finn said, "death would have occurred within an hour."

"I'm ruling this a suicide," Doc said. "I have no other evidence that points to anything different."

Alex nodded. "I agree. I just wish the note had been hand-written instead of typed."

"Poor Celeste," Finn said. "It'll take her a long time to get over this."

I nodded. "She was pretty devastated when we told her."

Finn rolled her head on her shoulders, cracking her neck. "What time are you going to Tommy's bar?"

My childhood friend, Tommy Trollman, owned a lively bar on the island called Boos & Brews. He'd offered to hold Serena's bachelorette party in his back room for us at no charge. He also said he'd throw in a few other freebies for us as well. I had no idea what that meant, but with Tommy, it could be anything. Alex wasn't a huge fan of Tommy's because sometimes Tommy had a tendency to blur the line when it came to the law.

"I'm going early to help decorate," I said. "I'll probably get there around seven."

"Is Needles going to the bachelorette party?" Finn asked.

Alex groaned. "Nope. Shayla is dropping him off at my house so he can go to the bachelor party, and she's picking up Zoie while there to help with the decorating. I obviously got the short straw in this deal."

I laughed. "Needles will love it. He has never attended a bachelor party. Just don't let him drink too much. He can't hold his liquor, and when drunk, he goes on and on about his warrior days. And then he'll challenge everyone to a sword fight."

Alex shook his head and closed his eyes while the rest of us laughed.

"We wanted Zoie to be able to participate as well," I said. "By letting her help decorate, and staying for a few minutes when it first starts, she can feel included."

"Well," Doc said, "I'm looking forward to the bachelor party. Guess I'll see you there around eight, Sheriff."

Finn crossed her arms over her chest. "Why did you guys decide on High Seas Bar & Grill for your bachelor party?"

"They have great food, and Zac has to work and tend bar until nine," Alex said. "He got us a great deal on the banquet room, plus he doesn't have far to go to get to the bachelor party."

Finn laughed. "Smart thinking."

W hat originally started out as ten of Serena's most intimate friends turned into a party of about sixty screaming women ranging in age from sixteen to ninety-six. Two different covens showed up, regular customers from the bakery, and pretty much every woman on the island who had heard whispers of the bachelorette party.

Aunt Starla, Mom, GiGi, Tamara, Zoie, and I worked tirelessly for an hour getting all the decorations up. Well, not too tirelessly when you take into account we'd used magic to hang most of the items. By the time nine o'clock rolled around, the party was in full swing, with drinks being consumed and music pumping.

"Who ordered the strippers?" Opal Earthly-Caraway cried out as she lifted her Blushing Bride drink in the air.

Pearl Earthly-Caraway grinned. "I hope they're the same ones we had at our bachelorette party, Sister!"

A round of cheers went up from the crowd of rowdy women.

Zoie laughed. "I think that's my cue to head on home. Brick,

Izzy, and Ty are dropping by around nine-thirty. We're gonna watch movies until Dad gets home. The guys' curfews have been extended for an hour since we are on winter break. So we might be able to squeeze in two movies."

"Thank you for all your help," I said, giving her a quick hug. "Have fun tonight. Drive home safe."

Zoie laughed. "I should say the same to you." She pointed to my drink. "You guys have a designated driver?"

"Mom is taking me and GiGi back to her place. Serena will stay with Aunt Starla."

"I hear Needles is spending the night with us," Zoie said. "Dad was super excited about it when he told me."

I threw back my head and laughed. "You're such a little liar."

"You're right." She gave me one more hug before picking up her purse across the room and heading out the back door of the bar.

"Oh, my goddess!" Serena exclaimed, wrapping her arms around my shoulder. "This is the best bachelorette party I could have ever hoped for."

I snorted. "Yeah, just ten of your closest friends."

Tamara sidled up next to us. "At least all these party crashers had the good sense to bring some food."

Serena nodded and sucked in another big breath to scream over the music. "And I still can't get over the fact Tommy Trollman is supplying eighty percent of the booze here tonight. That was so kind of him. Not only did he supply the venue, but he supplied the booze!"

The music had stopped right before Serena finished her sentence, so it sounded like she was shouting the word "booze" to the crowd.

"Booze!" several women shouted back, lifting their glasses in the air.

"This will definitely be a bachelorette party to remember," I said. "Maybe not as insane as the strippers at Opal's and Pearl's bachelorette party, but definitely remembered."

Tamara took a sip of her drink. "I wonder how our men are doing over at High Seas?"

"I wonder how Needles is doing?" I said with a laugh.

A couple of girls from the Singles coven ran over to us.

"You ladies need to dance!"

"And drink more!"

"This is a party!"

I laughed as the young girls dragged Serena and Tamara onto the dance floor. While I wasn't exactly old, at forty, I did have a harder time keeping up with the younger crowd. I held up my hand when they turned to me.

"I want to go thank Tommy for everything he supplied tonight," I said. "I'll be back in a few minutes."

I caught Mom's eyes across the crowded room and lifted my Blushing Bride drink in the air as a salute to her, Aunt Starla, and GiGi. As I turned toward the door that would lead out to the bar, I gave my head a small shake. I had to ask Tommy what was in the drink. I'd only had two, but I was definitely feeling it.

* * *

I let out a sigh of relief when I stepped into the bar. It was relatively quiet compared to the party going on in the back room. I made a beeline for Tommy's office, hoping that's where he'd be. When I reached his door, I knocked three times.

"C'mon in," a gruff voice called out.

I pushed open the door and smiled at Tommy, sitting behind his massive desk.

"Shayla Loci. What a surprise." Tommy stepped from behind

his desk and engulfed me in a hug. "I hope everything is going well in the back room. Plenty of drinks?"

I laughed and held up my Blushing Bride. "Plenty of drinks, Tommy. Thank you. I'm dying to know what's in this though." I took another sip. "Delicious."

Tommy laughed and patted my back with one of his beefy hands. "You be careful with those, little witch. The Blushing Bride has strawberry vodka, white rum, and just a splash of cherry 7-Up."

"No wonder two are about to put me under the table."

Tommy laughed. "Sit down. Sit down. What's up? I heard you had a big day finding Brody Lightweig dead. What a shame that is."

"Did you know him?" I narrowed my eyes. "Or should I say, did he owe you money?"

Tommy grinned. "No, he owed me no money. I don't loan to people like him."

I took a sip of my drink. "Whaddya mean? He had a good job. Surely if he needed a loan, he had collateral?"

Tommy steepled his fingers over his stomach and stared me in the eyes. "Rumor has it Brody was in major debt. He loved to gamble and play poker on the supernatural Internet, and he was a regular at back-room poker games around the island. Of course, that last part is just between us."

"Anyone on the island I need to look at that might have wanted him dead because of his debt?"

Tommy smiled. "The two or three he owed money to for gambling wouldn't kill him. Why would they? They'd never get their money. And it wasn't such a large amount that he would be worth killing. Hypothetically speaking."

"Uh-huh. But no names?"

Tommy laughed. "I can't get anything by you, Shayla Loci.

But don't worry. If I thought one of his collectors did this, I would tell you."

I took another sip of my drink and pretended the room wasn't tilting. "What about Garth Trollson? You know him?"

"I do. Comes in here quite often. He and his girlfriend both. In fact, I believe they're here now. Or at least they were when I did a walk through the bar about twenty minutes ago."

I raised an eyebrow. "Girlfriend? Do you know who she is?"

"I believe her name is LeeAnn something."

❧ 19 ❧

"What?" I demanded. "LeeAnn? As in LeeAnn Elmswood? That's his girlfriend?" I stood and quickly grabbed onto the chair so I wouldn't tip over. "She has some explaining to do."

Tommy stood and shook his head, smiling, as he maneuvered around his desk and wrapped an arm around my shoulders. "How about I go out there with you when you interrogate her?"

"You afraid I'm gonna get into a fight at your bar?" I joked.

"If I thought that, I'd be wagering a bet."

I poked him in the chest, and ended up hurting my finger. "Tommy Trollman, you know gambling is illegal."

Tommy laughed and guided me toward the door. "Always a stickler for the law, Shayla Loci. That's what I love about you."

We stepped out into the bar, and my eyes scanned the room. There were at least fifty people milling around, drinking, playing pool, and dancing to the music on the jukebox.

"Pretty tame for a Friday night," Tommy said. "But with the holidays upon us, it's not too surprising."

"I don't see them."

"Over in the corner booth. Come. Let's see how I do as your backup partner."

I tossed back the last of my Blushing Bride and set it down on a nearby table...ignoring the protests of the other patrons at the table.

Tommy chuckled and stopped a nearby waitress. "The next round is on the house for this table."

The grumbling immediately stopped, and cheers rang out among the four customers.

Tommy steered me over to the corner booth, where Garth and LeeAnn sat snuggled together, making cooing noises and drinking. I'm not sure why I was suddenly so pissed. After all, Brody had left a suicide note, and I had no proof these two had done anything wrong...but I was still miffed they were getting one over on Celeste.

I steadied myself on my feet. "Now I know why you didn't mention Garth Trollson leaving notes on the windshield of Celeste's car, LeeAnn, when I asked you if you knew of anyone wanting to hurt Celeste."

The couple sprang apart, and tears filled LeeAnn's eyes. "It's not like that! Please, don't tell Celeste about us until I have a chance to tell her. I've just been waiting for the right time."

I scoffed. "The right time? How long has this been going on?"

Garth reached out and grabbed LeeAnn's hand. "About three weeks. It's just as much a surprise for us, as it is for you and everyone else."

I drew my eyebrows together and frowned. Something still bothered me. Something about the notes and word choice. I closed my eyes and tried to grab onto the thoughts floating around in my head.

Deciding it might be better if I talked it out, I crossed my arms over my chest. "Some of the wording in the notes were different. Sometimes the person wrote out the word 'you,' and sometimes they made the letter 'u' in the text." I looked back and forth between the two of them—then dropped my arms in surprise when it finally came to me! "My gosh, LeeAnn, did you send threatening notes to Celeste as well?"

"What? No! Of course not! The notes were one of the reasons Garth and I had our first fight last week. Celeste got another note, but this one was really threatening. I blamed Garth, but he swears he never outright threatened her. Most of his notes were just demands that she sell to him."

"It's true," Garth said. "Mainly I was just being a pain in the ass, hoping she'd eventually get tired of it and sell to me. I never actually threatened her."

I shook my head. "Garth, I showed you one of the notes I found at Celeste's house. Did you or did you not write it? Because you told me you did."

Garth shrugged. "I assumed I did. I didn't know other people might send her notes as well. To be honest, I thought maybe LeeAnn had made a mistake when she said I left a note on Celeste's windshield. I thought maybe she had found one of the old notes I'd left in the yoga studio." He shrugged and gave me a sheepish look. "I didn't really want to press the issue. I just told LeeAnn I was sorry, and I wouldn't write notes anymore." He looked adoringly at LeeAnn. "I kinda like having them next door now. All that stuff I said about wanting the stretching place to go away…well, I kinda didn't mean it. I like having LeeAnn so close to me."

I rolled my eyes as the two of them made kissy-faces at each other. "I won't tell Celeste your secret right now, LeeAnn. But you both need to do it soon."

The couple both nodded.

"We promise, Shayla," LeeAnn said.

"Well, now," Tommy whispered in my ear, "that was anticlimactic. We didn't even get to hit anyone."

I laughed and turned back toward the back room. "Only you, Tommy. But it gives me a lot to think about. Something still doesn't sit right with me about Brody's suicide and Celeste's attempted murder."

Tommy stopped in front of the closed door that led to the bachelorette party. "Go have another drink and think about it. Just don't get hung up on it right now. Serena will only have one bachelorette party, and you need to enjoy this moment."

I stood on tiptoe and gave Tommy a kiss on the cheek. "You're a good friend, Tommy Trollman. Thanks for all you've done."

He gave me a grin. "Go have some fun, Shayla Loci. And give my best to the bride-to-be."

✿ 20 ✿

The bass pumped through my body as I crossed the crowded room and found GiGi. She was in a corner, hunched over her phone, texting.

"Since when do you text?" I asked, snagging another Blushing Bride off a passing tray.

"I've texted a time or two," GiGi snapped, shoving the phone in her pocket.

My eyes widened, and I couldn't help the grin that spread across my face. "Oh, my goddess! You're texting Byron Sealy, aren't you?" I gasped. "Were you *sexting*?"

"Hush your mouth, Shayla Loci. Or I'll turn you into a toad!"

I held up both hands, careful not to spill my delicious drink. "I got no beef with you, GiGi."

I took a drink and sighed. When no answers came to me about the investigation, I took another drink and sighed.

"Fine," GiGi said. "I'll ask. Why do you look like you just lost your favorite wand?"

"I'm trying to work out a couple things about the investigation."

"I thought the investigation was over? Brody wrote a letter admitting to poisoning Celeste, and then he killed himself by drinking the same poison. Case closed."

"I guess. But I just found out some new information that muddies the water a little bit. Or maybe it doesn't. I mean, maybe the notes that were so different on Celeste's car were because they were sent from two different people. I can now accept that fact. I thought for a moment they might be from LeeAnn, but maybe the threatening notes that spelled out words and didn't abbreviate and had proper grammar were from Brody Lightweig. His suicide note was written correctly." I took a drink and shook my head. "I just wished things fit into place better. I hate having unanswered questions."

GiGi cackled and took a sip of her own drink. "I only followed half of what you said. You can think about it tomorrow. You know, when you haven't had three or four of these fancy drinks." GiGi took another sip. "Speaking of fancy, have you seen some of the gifts Serena has received? The wrapping paper alone had to cost a pretty penny."

"What?" I set my drink down and shook my head to clear it. Something GiGi had just said triggered something in my brain. Something relevant to the case.

GiGi scowled. "I said the paper alone had to cost a pretty penny."

Facts and clues tumbled around drunkenly in my head...until they finally fell into place.

"That's it!" I grabbed GiGi's shoulders. "I need you to mix up one of your Sober Up Now elixirs. Can you do that?"

GiGi scoffed. "Why? We're having too much fun to sober up.

Your mom's the designated driver, so we can have as much booze and fun as we want tonight."

I shook my head. "This is important, GiGi. I think I figured something out, but I need to get to the sheriff's station real quick. I need to look at the evidence. Right now, neither one of us is sober enough to drive, *and* you don't exactly have a valid driver's license. I'm surprised Alex hasn't arrested you yet for driving your Vespa around the island."

GiGi snorted. "I'd like to see him try."

"GiGi, can you do it? Can you make the elixir?"

"Of course I can. But making the elixir isn't the hard part. The hard part is leaving without your mom or Serena seeing us. They aren't going to let us go on a wild goose chase tonight."

"I'll take care of the excuse. You just make the Sober Up Now."

GiGi grabbed a plastic martini glass off one of the nearby tables, then handed it to me. "You hold this, and I'll conjure up the ingredients. Let's turn our backs on everyone so they don't see what we're doing."

I turned around like she suggested, and watched in amazement as she started whispering the spell. Six bottles appeared out of thin air, and she carefully selected each one, pouring a different amount out of each bottle into the martini glass.

"How do you know how much to put in here?" I asked. "It's not like you have a measuring spoon."

"Either this will sober you right up, or you'll grow a tail, or your hair will fall out. But, we got a one in three chance, so I figure we're golden." GiGi cackled when she saw the look of horror on my face. "Lighten up, Shayla. I'm only joking. Sort of." She positioned her finger above the glass and twirled it counterclockwise three times. The liquid inside the glass moved in time with her finger. "There, it should be properly mixed. Bottoms up!"

I looked dubiously at the drink. "You're sure this will sober me up, right? I mean, I can't afford for my hair to fall out the night before Serena's wedding."

GiGi rolled her eyes. "Drink it."

Opening my mouth, I downed the liquid in one gulp... then shuddered as the bitterness of the drink coated my throat and stomach. But a few seconds later, the room was no longer tilting, and I didn't feel sluggish or disconnected.

"Perfect." I glanced over at GiGi, who was still chugging down her Blushing Bride. "Aren't you going to make you one so you can sober up?"

"Hell, no," GiGi said. "Everyone knows capturing a bad guy is always better when you're tipsy."

✤ 21 ✤

L uck was on our side. Gigi and I were able to sneak out the back door without anyone seeing us. Mom, Aunt Starla, and two other coven witches were busy laughing and chatting at a table. Serena, Tamara, and a group of their friends were on the dance floor, trying to teach the Earthly-Caraway twins naughty dance moves. No one gave us a second glance as we grabbed our purses, lifted Mom's keys, and hurried outside.

"Snow's coming down harder," GiGi said as she lifted something to her mouth. "You sure about this? It can't wait until morning?"

"I'm sure." I unlocked Mom's car, and we slid inside. "What are you drinking?"

GiGi gave me a tipsy grin, then lifted a bottle in the air. "I needed somewhere to put my drink. See, it's one of my potion bottles with a cork in the top."

I rolled my eyes as I started the car, flipped the heater on full blast, and headed toward the sheriff's station. "Wow, your Sober

Up Now potion really works. I feel more alert right now than I do most days."

"One of the first spells I perfected," GIGI said. "I don't know if you know this or not, but your mother and aunt were quite a handful growing up. I drank a lot." She took the cork out of her potion bottle and took a drink of the pink liquid. "And I just never stopped."

I laughed and parked in front of the station. There was a soft glow from the street lamps, but to make sure GiGi had plenty of light to see and not trip, I conjured up a light orb.

"Thanks, Shayla dear. Can't be too careful at my age." She pulled her coat tight against her and dropped her potion bottle in her purse. "Now, let's get inside before I freeze to death."

I looped my purse across my body and quickly keyed in the code to the door of the sheriff's station. The minute the door opened, a beeping from the alarm sounded, and I raced to shut it off.

"I want to set everything out into different piles," I said after disarming the alarm.

GiGi and I strolled over to the evidence room and carefully levitated all the evidence from the lockers and laid them out systematically.

"These are the threatening notes left on Celeste's car," I said. "As you can see, in some notes, words are spelled out, but in others, words are abbreviated or just the letter is used. Take this one." I levitated the note so it floated near GiGi's face. "There are at least three grammatical errors, and no punctuation. The letter 'u' is in place of the actual word. I mean, it's a mess. But look at this one." I levitated the note so GiGi could see the letter I'd found on Celeste's counter the day she was poisoned. "Everything looks good with this note. 'You will sell now if you know what's good for you!' Grammar is correct, and there are no short-ened words."

GiGi nodded her head. "Right. You've already established you believe there were two different people leaving the threat-ening notes. One was Garth Trollson, and you said the other one was Brody Lightweig."

"But look." From a different pile, I levitated a love letter I'd found in Celeste's dresser that Brody had written to Celeste. "I realize now what has been bothering me outside of the fact two different people wrote these notes. It's the paper. Feel the paper from the love letters Brody wrote to Celeste."

GiGi reached out and took the edge of the paper between her thumb and index finger and rubbed back and forth. "Okay. Feels like paper."

"Now, feel the paper from these grammatically correct threats that were left on Celeste's windshield."

I handed GiGi one of the notes, and again she took the edge of the paper between her thumb and index finger. Her eyebrows lifted in amazement as she realized what I was saying. "This paper is different. It's thicker. More expensive."

"Exactly. When you said tonight that Serena's gifts had fancy wrapping paper, that triggered me. If Brody was going to send love letters to Celeste, don't you think he'd use fancy paper? Instead, he saves the fancy paper for the threatening notes on her car? I don't think so." I took a deep breath. "GiGi, I don't think Brody left these threatening notes on Celeste's car. I also don't think Brody killed himself."

GiGi nodded gravely. "You think someone else broke into Celeste's house and left the poison in the jar and then later went to Brody's house and gave him the poison to drink?"

"That's exactly what I think. And I believe I know who the

killer is." I handed her a piece of paper from my purse. "Take a look at this."

✿ 22 ✿

"Are you sure we shouldn't just wait until tomorrow to confront her?" GiGi asked.

"Absolutely not. The last time we waited until morning, an innocent person—well, okay, maybe not an innocent person, but someone did die who didn't need to. Besides, tomorrow is Serena's wedding. No way am I ruining her wedding day. She'd never forgive me."

GiGi nodded and didn't say another word as I drove up the driveway. There were two lights on in the house, which I took to be a good sign.

"I can't believe I left my police-issued binder at Mom's," I grumbled.

"You were going to a bachelorette party," Gigi said. "What were you gonna do? Attach it to your bra?"

I smiled. "Yeah, it wasn't like I was expecting to need a weapon tonight."

"Don't worry. I got magic that can paralyze her if need be. We don't need no fancy police-issued binder." GiGi got out of

114

Mom's vehicle. "You know Alex is going to come undone when you call him and tell him you figured out who the killer is *and* you took her down without him. You ready for that fight?"

"You and I can handle this. You're the most powerful witch I know, and I trust you to have my back. Alex's ego isn't that fragile."

GiGi snorted as we walked up the sidewalk. "It's not his ego that I worry about. Don't pretend you don't know he's gonna be angry that you put yourself in this kind of danger without proper backup."

The overhead lights on the front porch illuminated GiGi's face.

"I know. But if I can't have Alex or Needles here, I really mean it when I say you are the best witch I know to have my back." I knocked twice on the door, then rang the doorbell. "I'll get her to confess, we'll take her down, and then transport her to the station."

GiGi snorted. "And we're gonna do all this with no plan?"

I was saved from answering as the front door swung open, and Laurel Muser stood in the doorway.

"Can I help you, ladies?" she asked.

"We need to ask you some questions," I said. "You don't mind if we come in, do you?"

She stared defiantly into my eyes. "Do I have a choice?"

"Not really," I said.

"Yeah, not really," GiGi echoed.

I did a quick visual scan of Laurel's body to see if she had any weapons on her. I didn't see any, but when she stepped back and motioned us inside, I never took my eyes off her.

"I'd offer you a place to sit, but I don't want you to think you're welcome here. I told you I'm very busy, and I don't have time for frivolous questions."

"I thought about it on the drive over," I said, "and there are still some pieces missing. I know Brody had a plan in place, one you denied knowing about. But I think that was a lie. I believe he concocted the original plan of leaving Celeste at the altar with you. Is that right?"

Laurel shrugged. "I will admit he and I concocted the plan for him to dump Celeste at the altar."

"Why? I mean, I know why you would want Celeste hurt, but why would Brody do it?"

Laurel let out a bark of laughter. "Because that idiot was in up to his neck in debt. I offered to pay off all his gambling debts, and in exchange, he would get Celeste Morningsong to fall in love with him."

"And then he'd bail out right before the wedding," GiGi said.

"That's quite devious," I said. "And petty."

"You're a witch. What do you know of the superiority of my people? Nothing. To you, I'm sure the challenge between the muses and the sirens is just another story. But to me, it's a way of life. No siren will ever get the best of me."

"But something changed," I said. "What was it?"

Laurel's nostrils flared, and she pinched her lips together. "Brody took a life insurance policy out on Celeste. She found out and called off the wedding! My idiot cousin couldn't even do one thing correct."

"So when you heard about the breakup," I said, "you knew that was your time to strike with the poison. If Celeste died, Brody would be the first person the police looked at."

Laurel shrugged. "I don't suppose it will hurt to admit I knew Celeste's schedule, thanks to Brody. I knew she worked Sundays and then went to her sister's for dinner. I won't deny that. And perhaps I knew that the roommate also worked most Sunday evenings. But how did I get inside?"

I rolled my eyes. "You just said Brody told you about Celeste's Sunday schedule. I'm sure he also told you about the hidden key in the backyard."

"Perhaps," Laurel said. "But there's no evidence pointing to me that says I went inside Celeste's house and dumped the ground up water hemlock into the glass jar sitting on the counter."

"I never said where the poison was located," I said. "In fact, Alex and I made it a point to leave that part out."

GiGi cackled. "Gotcha!"

Laurel clenched her fists at her side. "It's still just conjecture. You have no physical proof."

I gave her a tight smile. "That's where you're wrong. Remember the paper you gave me with your lawyer's information? Well, it's a match for the paper you used to write Celeste threatening notes. That's more than just coincidence." I walked over to her coat closet and opened the door. "And what do we have here? A black coat with faux white fur. I have a witness statement placing you at Celeste's house Sunday wearing the same jacket."

I didn't feel the need to tell her the coat thing was pretty weak since a lot of women had the same one. What she didn't know wouldn't hurt her.

"Gotcha again!" GiGi exclaimed.

"What about the poison Brody ingested?" I asked.

Laurel cocked her head and eyed me coolly. "I may have called him over here Thursday around five for him to get his yearly Yule gift. I always got him the same thing—a nice pricy bottle of bourbon." She smiled. "I did warn him to drink it slowly because the bourbon may one day be the death of him." She laughed. "I felt it a fitting warning."

"And then what?" I mused. "You drove to his house in the

middle of the night and left the suicide note where we'd find it."

"That's exactly what I did. I knew there was no way he wouldn't drink most of the bottle that night. So I made sure to triple the poison amount. I waited until about three in the morning, used the key he hid under a flower pot in his front yard, saw he was dead, then dropped the note on the end table. Easy as that."

"You're one twisted lady," GiGi said. "But maybe you can see a shrink when you're rotting in your prison cell."

I let out a bark of laughter. Leave it to GiGi to have the last snide word.

"Now," GiGi said, "you're gonna come with us so we can take you in and get back to our party. Although, it's getting late enough now, I doubt we can go back."

Laurel let out a snort of laughter. "Oh, I'm not going anywhere with you two."

GiGi smirked and put her hands on her hips. "Oh, really? We're witches, and you're a muse. Whaddya gonna do? Write us to death?"

"No," Laurel said as she whipped out a gun from behind her back and pointed it in our general direction. "I just plan on shooting you both."

I was about to throw up a shield, when GiGi waved her hand through the air and caused the gun to fly out of Laurel's grasp. But not before Laurel got off a shot.

GiGi cried out in pain, and for a moment, I was paralyzed with fear. But then impulse took over, and I dived at Laurel. We both went down to the ground, grappling to get on top…but I had the physical advantage. I quickly conjured up a pair of handcuffs, flipped her over, and clamped them tightly over her wrists.

"Looks like I'll be putting that call into Alex now," I said. "And maybe an ambulance? How badly are you hurt?"

GiGi scoffed. "It's just a graze. Your mom and I can whip up a poultice to put on it tonight. It doesn't even need stitches."

I groaned as I forced Laurel to stand. "You realize it's not just Alex and Needles who are going to be mad at us, right? Mom, and Starla, and even Serena will probably lecture us all night and into the early morning hours."

GiGi cackled. "Good thing I got an endless supply of that Blushing Bride drink in my potion bottle."

* * *

"What on earth were you two thinking?" Alex demanded.

"Yes! What were you thinking, Princess?"

Instead of pacing back and forth in the air, Needles was weaving drunkenly through the air, his red wings barely fluttering enough to keep him afloat. *"You could have been killed."* Needles stopped trying to pace and just swayed in the air. *"Black Forest King would never have let me live it down."*

"You're right, Needles," I said, trying not to laugh.

Both the bachelor and bachelorette parties had shut down the minute I called Alex and Mom. The former sheriff, Walt Hawkins, drove Alex, Grant, Doc, and Needles to Laurel's place, while Mom gathered up Aunt Starla and Serena and called an Uber. She was not happy I'd taken her car.

It had taken some convincing for Alex not to call out the ambulance for GiGi, but when Doc proclaimed it was just a superficial wound, and Mom reassured Alex she and Aunt Starla could handle the doctoring, he finally relented.

"I agree with Needles," Mom said. "I'm so mad right now, Shayla, I could zap you and GiGi into next Tuesday."

GiGi took a healthy drink from her potion bottle. "It was all Shayla's idea. You should be mad at just her."

"Thanks, GiGi," I said dryly. "I knew you'd have my back."

"At least the real killer has been caught," Serena said. "That's a relief."

"And it wasn't like I didn't have a plan," I said. "I didn't want to wait until tomorrow and ruin the wedding, so GiGi and I decided to bring Laurel in tonight."

Needles landed on my shoulder and hiccupped. *"But you did it without me. You know the rule, Princess. Where you go, I go."*

"I know. And I'm sorry, Needles. How about I make it up to you with the bag of pretzels?"

"With caramel dip?"

I laughed. "Deal."

Needles flew from my shoulder, his wings a kaleidoscope of colors. *"Then I declare I am no longer angry with you."*

Alex narrowed his eyes at me and crossed his massive arms over his chest. "It's gonna take more than a bag of pretzels and caramel dip for me not to be angry that you recklessly put your life in danger."

"And my life!" GiGi piped in before taking another drink from her bottle. "Don't forget, my life was in danger as well."

I scowled at GiGi, then turned to Alex. "I know. And I'll think of a way to make it up to you."

He unfolded his arms and drew me to his side. "You do that." He kissed my temple. "You girls go on home. Deputy Sparks should be here any minute. Grant and I will follow him back to the station and make sure Laurel is locked up tight."

"I already called Zane," I said. "He informed me he was on assignment and couldn't pick Laurel up tomorrow, but he'd let the agency know and someone will be here in the morning to collect her."

"Then I say we go home." GiGi lifted her almost-empty potion bottle in the air. "I'm about out of that scrumptious drink, and I need my beauty sleep. I got me a granddaughter to marry off tomorrow."

❧ 23 ❧

"Y ou look gorgeous, Serena." I clinked my champagne glass with hers. "I can't believe in just a few minutes, you're gonna be walking down that aisle."

"I can't believe in less than half an hour, I'm gonna be Serena Spellburn-Wolfe."

"I just spoke with Mom," Tamara said as she sidled up next to us. "She just finished placing the cake on the table. You can take a quick peek."

The three of us walked to the window from inside our second-story suite at The Spellmoore and looked out onto the back of the resort. Snow was once again falling, but the guests sitting in the chairs facing the archway of flowers couldn't feel a thing thanks to Mom and two other witches in the coven. They'd erected an invisibility shield around where the wedding and reception would take place—next to the outdoor pond.

The four-tiered wedding cake sat majestically in the center of the reception table. Next to that was another table piled high with serving tiers filled with cupcakes and cookies. Red and green lights twinkled high in the air above the shield. Red in honor of Serena's dragon heritage on her dad's side, and green in honor of her witch heritage on Aunt Starla's side.

"It's beautiful," Serena whispered. "I couldn't have asked for a more perfect winter wedding."

There was a sharp knock on the door before it swung open. GiGi stood in the doorway clad in her best ritual robe. "I hear there's a witch needing to be married."

We all laughed and motioned her inside.

"I've spoken with Grant," GiGi said. "He and his men are ready."

Serena drained the last of her champagne. "Then I'm ready as well."

"Walt is downstairs by the back door, eager to walk you down the aisle," GiGi said. "Celeste is at the microphone ready to sing, and Zoie is as nervous as a cat in a room full of rocking chairs. But she swears she's ready to light all twelve candles at once."

I grinned. "We've been practicing for weeks now. She can do it."

Serena picked up her bridal bouquet. "Let's go get me hitched."

* * *

The wedding was perfect. Zoie used her magic and lit all twelve candles at once, Celeste's songs were stunning, and GiGi conducted a flawless service. I cried a lot, but I knew I would.

"Have I told you how beautiful you look tonight?" Alex whispered in my ear as we swayed slowly back and forth on the dance floor.

I leaned back and smiled. "Only like six or seven times. But I like hearing it."

He whirled me around, and my breath hitched. "Good. Because I like saying it."

"Can you believe GiGi is out here dancing with Byron Sealy?" I grinned. "I knew if he kept trying, she'd eventually give in."

Alex grunted. "Someone should warn that poor selkie."

I threw back my head and laughed. "Something tells me he knows exactly what he's getting into." I let my eyes travel over the other dancers. "Zoie looks happy."

Alex followed my gaze to where Zoie and Brick were dancing and groaned. "She looks so grown up." His brow furrowed. "Are they dancing too close? I think they might be. I should probably go over there and break them—"

I put my hand on his cheek and physically drew his gaze back to me. "Do not tell me you are so old you don't remember being their age?"

Alex scowled. "That's what scares me."

Grinning, I pulled him down and kissed him lightly on the mouth. "You're an amazing father, Alex Stone. Trust her to find her own way."

The music ended, and Alex and I walked back to where Mom and Aunt Starla sat, drinking and laughing with Walt.

Needles zipped over to us, his wings a vibrant purple. *"Black Forest King's surprise is ready, Princess."*

I caught Serena's eyes across the lawn and motioned her and Grant over.

"What's going on?" Serena asked.

"My dad has a surprise for you," I said.

"Do you know what it is?" Grant asked.

I grinned. "Yep. You both need to look to the north…high in

the sky. While Dad said it was for you both, he especially wanted Serena to know he was thinking of her and her father on this day."

A few seconds later, red and green and white fireworks filled the sky. All the guests stopped to watch the beautiful display of lights and sound. A rumble of excitement ran through the crowd as Randor took to the sky, seeming to fly effortlessly between the lights.

Serena sniffed and wiped at her eyes. "Randor represents my dad, right?"

"Yeah," I whispered.

Serena wrapped her arms around me and rested her head on my shoulder. "Tell Black Forest King it was the perfect gift."

❦ 24 ❦

"*I do not want to keep you,*" Dad said. *"If you two must leave, I understand."*

"Serena and Grant aren't due back to the island from their honeymoon for another hour," I said, my back pressed against Dad's trunk. "Alex and I have plenty of time. Although, it'll be weird visiting her in a new home."

Grant and Serena had decided to move into Grant's place in town and give Tamara the cottage. Tamara had three different gardens planted around the cottage—each for specific purposes. Serena didn't think it fair to ask Tamara to move and start the gardens over from scratch.

In the two weeks Grant and Serena and been gone, I'd nearly went out of my mind. I hadn't realized how much of an impact they had on my everyday life until they weren't there. While I had a friendship with Tamara, it was nothing like my friendship with my cousin. My daily trips to the bakery seemed hollow without her.

"I am sorry you will not get to meet Alex's family when you travel to Seattle next week," Dad said.

"Me too," Alex said. "Who knew my parents would plan a supernatural cruise the same week we were scheduled to be in Seattle?"

"But it won't be a wasted trip," I said. "I'll finally get to meet his ex-partner, Kara Hilder."

"And you claim she is not a supernatural, Alex Stone?" Dad mused.

"Not that I'm aware, and not that she's aware," Alex said. "Trust me, that's something I'm sure she would have shared with me. And I never picked up on it. I mean, she knows multiple fighting techniques, but I never saw anything supernatural about her fighting."

Alex's cell phone rang, and his eyes widened. "Speaking of Kara." He slid his finger over the green phone and lifted it to his ear. "Hello, Kara. Shayla and I were just talking about you." He paused and frowned. "Hold on. Slow down. Say that again? You're with Zane? Like Shayla's ex-partner, Zane?" Alex listened for a while longer, then he suddenly stood and stumbled backward, his face deathly white. "What? You're sure? We'll be there as quickly as we can."

Alex disconnected and rested his hands on his knees.

"What's wrong?" I stood and placed my hands on his back. "Did Kara say she was with Zane?"

Alex stood and took a deep breath. "This is unbelievable. Kara said she's working with Zane on a case to find a killer, and she just learned from her grandmother—who happens to be Rota Gunner, by the way—that she's a Valkyrie. Oh, and she said she also has the ability to do magic, but it's wonky still. Whatever that means?"

"Rota is her grandma?" I shook my head in disbelief. "That's crazy. I mean, I knew Rota had a daughter, but…" My voice trailed off as memories about Rota and her daughter flooded me. "How did Zane put it together that Kara and Rota were related?"

Alex shrugged. "I don't know exactly, but I guess Zane found Kara in Seattle a couple days ago and took her to a town called Mystic Cove."

"Mystic Cove is where Zane, Rota, and I were based out of," I said. "We helped police the town when we weren't on an assignment for the government."

"But something is still wrong," Dad said. *"You do not look well, Alex Stone."*

Alex grabbed hold of my hand. "You're right, sir. Kara said Shayla and I need to get to Mystic Cove immediately."

"Whoohoo!" Needles cried. *"Good thing I already have my suitcase packed."*

"Why do we need to go to them?" I asked, ignoring Needles. "Can't she and Zane handle the case themselves? I've never known Zane to need extra help."

Alex shook his head. "You don't understand. Kara said one of the suspects is my ex-wife." He closed his eyes. "After all these years, Camille has finally surfaced. This is going to devastate Zoie."

I knew he was right. Zoie and I had spoken extensively about her mother, and Zoie's resentment toward her mother for abandoning them. In fact, Zoie had searched both the supernatural internet and human internet hoping to find out anything about Camille. This news would cut Zoie to the core.

I grabbed Alex's hand. "Then we pack tonight, and leave in the morning. We can be in Mystic Cove by sundown."

* * *

Ready for Book 11, Deadly Doctor, in the A Witch in the Woods series? Click here: My Book

* * *

How about a sneak peek of the NEW Kara Hilder Mystery series? Read Chapter 1 of Sounds of Murder. Then grab the link at the end of the chapter!

"Happy birthday to me."

I caught the bartender's eyes, lifted my empty glass, and signaled for one more. Usually I was a one-and-done kind of girl, but today was my fortieth birthday, and it wasn't like there was anyone waiting for me at home. Not on two legs, anyway. My cat, Savage, was probably taking his perpetual grumpy mood out on the left-over Christmas and New Year's decorations I still had up around my otherwise sparse apartment.

It was still early for a Friday night, barely six o'clock. I'd have one more drink and then head to my place to wallow in self-pity the rest of the night.

Normally, my ex-partner, Alex Stone, and his teenaged daughter, Zoie, would treat me to a birthday dinner. But Alex had moved from Seattle a year ago, so the only communication I had with him now was over the phone. I once tried to locate exactly where he'd moved to, but when I told him I couldn't find Enchanted Island anywhere on the map, he said the place was too small. It still baffled me as to why he'd give up a career as a detective with the Seattle Police Department to move to some tiny island and be their new sheriff.

"What kind of name is Enchanted Island, anyway?" I mumbled into my empty drink.

A body pressed up against me, but I didn't even acknowledge the guy—even though the scent of his soap was divine. "Excuse me? My name is Zane. I was hoping to buy you another drink so we can talk for a few moments."

I barely refrained from rolling my eyes. As far as pick-up lines went, it definitely wasn't offensive, but I wasn't in the mood to play nice. I didn't even turn to look at him, just stared into my drink. "Look, Zane, I'm just here to have a drink. Go pedal your wares somewhere else."

The man laughed, and I turned to glare at him—and did a double-take. He was hands down the sexiest man I'd ever seen. And that was saying a lot, considering my ex-partner usually held that honor. Dark hair, darker eyes, prominent nose, dazzling smile, and what I figured was a permanent five o'clock shadow. He was also dressed in an expensive suit and tie. A first for this dive bar, I was sure.

"My wares?" Zane said. "I assure you, Kara, I am not trying to pick you up."

I narrowed my eyes. "How do you know my name?"

"If you'll give me a moment of your time, I will tell you."

The bartender set my whiskey in front of me, and I turned back to thank him. As the barkeep walked away, I reached down and pushed my leather jacket aside, exposing my detective's badge. "I mean it, pal. Back off. Or I will arrest you."

"As entertaining as that might be," Zane said, "I'm afraid I must insist."

"That's where you're wrong." I took a long swallow of my whiskey and tried not to shudder as it burned a path down my throat to my stomach. I definitely needed to splurge next time and go for the more expensive stuff. "Now, if you'll excuse me, I need to go."

I grabbed my purse, tossed out enough bills to pay for the two drinks and leave a nice tip, and walked away without looking back.

Pushing open the restroom door, I headed for the sink. Splashing water on my face, I looked in the mirror and assessed myself. Cornflower blue eyes, smooth skin with no signs of wrinkles yet—which was something—narrow nose, full lips, and a body I keep trim with daily martial arts. The haphazard knot on top of my head was slipping, so I withdrew the bobby pins and elastic band, shook it free, then quickly plaited the long, blonde hair loosely down the back of my head, before securing it once again with the elastic band.

Blotting my face dry, I threw away the paper towel and headed outside to my dilapidated car I prayed made it one more year. I couldn't afford a new one just yet. Budgeting was hard to do on a detective's salary.

With keys in hand, I strode across the bar's parking lot. I was almost at my vehicle when I heard a noise behind me. Without thinking, I whirled around and kicked out at my assailant…and was momentarily stunned when the guy blocked my kick effortlessly with his forearm.

Straightening, I sent a jab to his face with my right hand… and again he blocked me.

"I can do this all night, little warrior," Zane said. "But I prefer not to. Your grandmother, Rota Gunner, is eager to meet you."

I blinked in surprise. "My grandmother? I don't have a grandmother. I was abandoned as a child. Not that it's any of your business."

"That's where you're wrong, Kara. You *do* have a grandmother, and she's a Valkyrie, just like you. She's been eager to meet you ever since she found out about you."

"Enough! I told you to leave me alone. If you insist on playing up this rouse, I *will* make you regret it."

Zane sighed. "I just want you to remember that I tried many times to do this the easy way, but you stubbornly refused. Not that I should be surprised. It's a trait your grandmother and you share."

Whoosh!

I was about to reach for my concealed gun when I froze. The devilishly handsome man in front of me was now sporting the largest pair of black wings I'd ever seen.

* * *

I groaned…then winced when the sound echoed loudly in my head. Forcing my eyes open, I scrambled to sit up in the seat. "Where am I? Where are you taking me? Kidnapping a police officer will get you countless years in prison, pal."

"Relax, Kara, you are perfectly safe."

"I'm expected back on duty Sunday," I said. "If I don't report in, you'll have dozens of cops after you."

"You'll need to call in to your precinct tomorrow and ask for time off," Zane said.

I snorted. "The heck I will." I threw up my hands. "I can't even believe I'm having a somewhat rational conversation with you right now about kidnapping me!"

"It's not kidnapping," Zane said smoothly. "I'm simply taking you to see your grandmother on your birthday."

I closed my eyes and leaned back in the seat, doing my best to block out my captive's ridiculous ramblings. I had to get it together and figure out a way to escape. My hand crept to my back, where I kept my concealed gun when I was off duty. It was gone.

"I didn't want you to shoot me on accident," Zane said. "Not to worry, you can have it back when we get to where we're going."

"I hope I don't accidentally shoot you then."

Zane laughed. "You're funny, valiant warrior. Now, just sit back and relax. The '65 Aston is a most pleasant ride, I can assure you."

Ignoring him, I ran my hand over the expensive tan leather interior of the sports car. I'd seen pictures and watched movies with vintage Aston Martins, but I'd never actually sat in one. Some of them went for over three hundred thousand dollars!

"If you're cold," Zane continued, "I can put the top up. I almost always drive with it down for my own pleasure. But if you're cold, I can—"

"Stop talking to me. I can't deal with your level of crazy right now."

Zane chuckled, but wisely kept his mouth shut.

"I need to be back tomorrow," I said. "I have a cat who depends on me to feed him. And trust me, you don't want to see him angry. Or better yet…hangry. He lives up to his name."

"All right, I'll bite. What's your cat's name?"

"Savage," I said. "On really ornery days, it's Savage Beast."

Zane laughed. "Why am I not surprised you'd own an angry, fighting cat?"

Ignoring the taunt, I glanced around and tried to find familiar markers that would tell me how long I'd been out. But I didn't recognize the landscape outside. It was too dark to see much, but from what I could tell, we were in the middle of nowhere on a two-lane road surrounded by trees and open land. Definitely not in downtown Seattle anymore.

"We're almost there, Kara," Zane said.

"How did I get here?" I asked.

"I flew you. It was quicker for me to use my wings and fly to where you'd be tonight than to drive the Aston to Seattle. So once I left Mystic Cove, I drove to the nearest abandoned warehouse in your world, parked the Aston, and flew to you."

"My world?" I snorted. "Are you from outer space, then?"

Zane gave me a 'get real' look before turning his attention back to the road. "No, I'm not from outer space, but I am from a world you don't know. I'm a supernatural, Kara. Just like your grandmother."

I frowned. "A supernatural? Like that show on TV about the two brothers who hunted down demons and stuff?"

"Something like that. In my world there are witches, vampires, merpeople, pixies, werewolves, dragons, and all—"

"Stop right there." I threw up my hand. "I don't want to hear another outrageous lie from your mouth."

Your lying, crazy, beautiful mouth.

"You don't remember coming to while we were still in the air flying? You freaked out and started screaming, and then you passed out when I did a little nose dive." Zane chuckled. "I expected more from a Valkyrie. You know there was a time when Valkyrie's rode the skies on their winged horses, right?"

"A what? What're you talking about?" I waved my hand again in the air. "Never mind. The less I know, the better." I turned in my seat and stared at him. "Were you just released from a mental health facility?"

Zane scoffed. "I'm offended by that question, Kara. You know what you saw. You just can't admit it right now. But soon you will. We're almost home."

"Uh, I already have a home, and I'm not looking to join your little cult and mingle with your twenty wives as we sell fruit on the side of the road."

Zane threw back his head and laughed. "I find I enjoy your humor, warrior."

"Lucky me," I muttered.

Zane downshifted and made a left turn onto a narrow lane that actually had grass poking out of the dirt and rocks.

"Um, Zane? I don't think this is right. The sign back there said this was a no outlet road."

Zane didn't say anything as we bumped slowly down the lane. There was no longer a road to speak of, just grass and trees. When his headlights focused in on a massive tree in the middle of the road, I expected him to stop and turn around.

He didn't. He just kept driving.

I grabbed hold of the dashboard. "Are you crazy? That's a tree in front of us! You need to stop and turn around."

"Trust me, Kara."

I opened my mouth to scream as we plowed head-first into the tree...and passed right through, exiting onto a paved road that led to a brightly lit seaside town less than half a mile away.

"Welcome to Mystic Cove," Zane said.

* * *

D on't forget to buy book 1, Sounds of Murder, in the new supernatural cozy mystery series, A Kara Hilder Mystery! Click here to read the rest of the story: My Book

* * *

Do you love the idea of a time-traveling, cold-case solving witch? Then Lexi and her side-kick detective familiar, Rex the Rat, are just what you're looking for! Check out their first stop to 1988 in Time After Time My Book

Have you read the hilarious adventures of Ryli Sinclair and Aunt Shirley? Book 1 is Picture Perfect Murder! My Book

Love the idea of a bookstore/bar set in the picturesque wine country of Sonoma County? Then join Jaycee, Jax, Gramps, Tillie, and the whole gang as they solve murders while slinging suds and chasing bad guys in this hilarious series. My Book

How about a seaside mystery? My stepdaughter and I write a mystery where high school seniors pair up with their grandma and great-aunt! Book one, Seaside & Homicide: My Book

Or maybe you're in the mood for a romantic comedy...heavy on comedy and light on sweet romance? Then the Trinity Falls series is for you! My Book

. . .

L ooking for a paranormal cozy series about a midlife witch looking to make a new start with a new career? Then A Witch in the Woods is the book series for you! A game warden witch, a talking/flying porcupine, and a gargoyle sheriff! My Book

ABOUT THE AUTHOR

Jenna writes in the genres of cozy/paranormal cozy/ romantic comedy. Her humorous characters and stories revolve around over-the-top family members, creative murders, and there's always a positive element of the military in her stories. Jenna currently lives in Missouri with her fiancé, step-daughter, Nova Scotia duck tolling retriever dog, Brownie, and her tuxedo-cat, Whiskey. She is a former court reporter turned educator turned full-time writer. She has a Master's degree in Special Education, and an Education Specialist degree in Curriculum and Instruction. She also spent twelve years in full-time ministry.

When she's not writing, Jenna likes to attend beer and wine tastings, go antiquing, visit craft festivals, and spend time with her family and friends. Check out her website at http://www.jennastjames.com/. Don't forget to sign up for the newsletter so you can keep up with the latest releases! You can also friend request her on Facebook at jennastjamesauthor/ or catch her on Instagram at authorjennastjames.

Made in United States
North Haven, CT
31 December 2024

63789170R00078